I0589774

CYNTHIA HICKEY

Poison Foliage

A Shady Acres Mystery, Book 3

By Cynthia Hickey

ISBN-13: 978-1-0881-3853-3

1

"*I* am getting very tired of renting the same cottages over and over." Alice Johnson, the manager of Shady Acres, plopped into a chair next to me, Shelby Hart. "I mean, seriously. Between deaths and murderers, all of which started occurring after I hired you, this place is a revolving door."

Seriously? How could she possibly think any of this was my fault?

Alice sipped her iced tea. "Now that the apartments in the main building are renovated, we can fill those rooms and the empty cottages." Her eyes shined. "With everything together, we have one hundred places to rent."

"You've done a good job as manager here." I glanced to where Heath filled his plate at the buffet. Not only was he the handsomest man in Arkansas, but he was also my boyfriend and had helped get me out of more than one tight spot in the last year.

I cut my fork into runny eggs and grimaced. The new cook left a lot to be desired in her culinary skills.

"This is awful." Alice tossed down a bread roll. "I must speak with the chef immediately." Without an "excuse me" or "goodbye" she headed for the kitchen.

Considering the sentiments from the residents echoing around the dining room, more than one person agreed with Alice and I on the quality of the food.

"Good morning, beautiful." Heath sat in the chair Alice had vacated. "What's wrong?"

"The new chef is terrible." I shoved my plate away.

"Maybe she just needs to settle in." Always the optimist, Heath took a healthy serving of clumpy oatmeal. "Yuck."

"See?" I crossed my arms and stared toward the kitchen as cries of outrage grew louder.

I loved the residents of Shady Acres, I truly did, but one thing falls out of place or the quality slips, and they were quick to riot. I watched as Bob Satchett, ringleader of the Poker Boys, stormed to the kitchen right along with his four cohorts and a new resident by the name of Lloyd Dane. I hadn't met Lloyd yet, but his salt and pepper hair and haughty attitude had the single golden ladies in a whirl.

"I am going to waste away with this slop." Grandma, skinny to the point of being blown away, followed by my much quieter mother, joined us at the table.

"Unless you're willing to cook, hush," Mom said.

"Easy for you to say. You haven't taken a bite yet." Grandma frowned and reached for her water goblet. "I'll get something in my cabin."

Mom shrugged. "What's on the agenda today, Shelby? I have some phone calls to make. Alice said once all the cottages and rooms are rented, I can have a raise."

"I have some work to do in the vegetable garden." Not to mention another weekly social. I was to the point where we were going to have to repeat some of our earlier activities. As gardener and event coordinator, don't forget Alice's personal assistant, I had more work than time. So, Mom felt compelled to lessen my load when she could. "You make your calls. My day is light."

She narrowed her eyes. "Are you just saying that?"

"Nope. Honest." Some weeding in the vegetable garden, some herbs to cut, then a ride around the grounds in my new golf cart to make sure nothing was amiss, and I was good to go.

"I'm painting the last of the upstairs apartments," Heath said. "Then, you can start filling them up, Sue Ellen."

I gave Heath a quick kiss, then set my plate on the sideboard. I grabbed what looked like a crescent from a can and munched on it as I made my way to the garden.

Passing the pool area, I glanced through the gate. "Mornin' Ted."

"Mornin'. Looking for trouble?" Former police officer, now retired, Ted Lawrence couldn't resist bringing up the mysteries I'd gotten involved in in the past. "If you see Ida, tell her I'm waiting."

Did I mention he dated my Grandmother and had moved into one of the cottages? "She's at breakfast." I waved and continued on my way.

Late summer and the sun was already hot on my

head as I knelt in the dirt and pulled weeds. I slowly made my way toward my herbs, noting a fresh patch of dirt. Something had been planted recently, and not by me. I eyed the parsley looking plant. Something the cook needed? One of the residents?

The garden was there for kitchen, staff, and residents. It wasn't unheard of for me to run across something I hadn't planted. I shrugged and let the plant be.

Loud voices across the way had me peering over the hedge like a nosey old woman. Our over-weight, five foot ten inch chef, Joyce Rhodes was staring down at pink-haired Birdie Sorenson as if she wanted to stomp the smaller woman into the ground.

Birdie planted her fists on her tiny hips and glared. "It ain't my fault you cook worse than a five-year-old."

"I spent years—*years*—in culinary school. How dare you!" Joyce's face reddened.

"Nobody likes the food you cook. Why, I saw those men march into the kitchen."

"Men, pshaw!" Joyce spit. "Not worth the gold in their teeth. Any of them. The world would be better off without them."

I tended to disagree. I rather liked men. Before the two women could come to blows, I stepped from around the hedge. "Hello." I pasted on my cheesiest, er, cheeriest, grin.

"Butt out, Shelby." Birdie turned her wrath on me.

"What did I do?" I held up my hands.

"You're going to tell me to be nice."

"You're entitled to your opinion."

"Great." Joyce turned toward the pool. "Here comes the cop." She whirled and stormed back to the main building.

"Ladies." Ted cocked his head. "Everything all right?"

"Peachy." Birdie marched away.

I looked at Ted and shrugged. "Difference of opinion on the food."

"Hmm." He glanced in the direction the women had gone. "Not boring around here, that's for sure."

"Not for long anyway." I said goodbye and headed for my storage shed.

More of the strange parsley had been planted along the side. Strange. There was plenty of room in the garden. I bent and plucked one from the ground, noting the radish shaped roots. It had to be a weed. I'd never seen an herb of its type before…or a vegetable.

I pulled up the plants and tossed them in a nearby garbage can before retrieving my golf cart. Moments later, floppy straw hat low on my head, I set off at the speed of ten miles per hour. Barely enough to cause a breeze strong enough to cool me off.

Mr. Dane stumbled in front of me, bent over and clutching his stomach. I hit the brakes and put the cart in park. I jumped from the vehicle and rushed to his side.

"Are you all right, Mr. Dane?"

"Call me Lloyd. We're both adults." Perspiration dotted his forehead. He moaned and swayed. "That woman's awful cooking. I bet I have food poisoning."

"Hop in. I'll give you a ride to your cottage. Or would you rather go to the hospital?"

"I've some antacid in my room. That ought to take care of the problem."

Praying he wouldn't vomit in my ride, I helped him

onto the seat, placed in hand in the "Oh, no!" strap, and sped at twelve miles per hour toward his cottage. Surely, Alice would forgive the two miles over her self-imposed speed limit.

Lloyd was gasping for breath by the time I helped him to his sofa. I grabbed the wall phone and dialed 911.

I knew the symptoms of food poisoning and this wasn't it.

Lloyd was bent double in pain, breathing in short gulps of air. "Everything is blurry. I ache all over."

The flu maybe? I rushed to get him a drink of water, keeping the phone to my ear as the 911 operator instructed. Ted arrived before the ambulance.

He burst into the cottage. "I heard the scanner." He knelt next to Lloyd. "Can you hear me?"

"I ain't deaf. Just sick." Lloyd closed his eyes. "Real sick."

"What have you eaten or drank?"

"Nothing since that mess at breakfast."

That was hours ago. "He thought he might have food poisoning," I said.

"No food poisoning I ever saw," Ted said, standing.

"Paramedics are here." I stood back as two men rushed forward and helped Lloyd onto a gurney.

"I'll go with them. Tell Ida where I've gone."

I nodded, knowing Alice would spit nails if I didn't tell her, too. "I hope you're better soon, Lloyd."

He waved a hand in response as he was wheeled out the door just as the lunch bell rang. I sighed and headed for the dining room.

The place was half full. It seemed as if most of the

residents had chosen to eat in their homes. A pity, considering the three buffet meals a day were included in the price of their rent.

"Shelby." Grandma rushed toward me. "Ted just called me. Put that sandwich down or you'll be in the hospital with Lloyd."

I eyed the ham and cheese. "It looks like it's fine."

She slapped it down. "You mind me."

Sighing, I tossed the sandwich in the garbage. "What am I supposed to eat?"

"I've several frozen dinners at my place. You'll join me, Sue Ellen, and Heath."

Gross. I hated processed food. "Just this once."

She wagged a finger in my face. "You'll eat what I serve until that chef is replaced."

Feeling like a scolded child, I followed her to her cottage. Laughter rang out before we'd opened the door. Dressed in a frilly red apron, Heath stood at the stove, spatula in hand.

"Omelets for lunch." He grinned and slid one on the plate.

"You're amazing." I gave him a warm kiss and carried my treasure to the table.

"I know you aren't a fan of frozen meals."

"What's wrong with them?" Grandma glowered.

"They aren't good for you, Grandma." I cut into an omelet with bacon, cheese, mushrooms, and spinach.

"Who says? I'm the picture of good health. Sue Ellen?"

"Sorry, Mother, I'm having a vegetable omelet." She took the plate offered by Heath.

"Do eggs go with wine?" Grandma pouted.

"They go great with mimosas." Heath handed her a

fluted glass of champagne and orange juice.

"Hold on to him, Shelby. He knows what a girl wants when she wants it." Grandma lifted the glass to her lips.

I smiled over her head at Heath. Grandma was right. He was a true treasure. One I'd almost let go out of distrust of men. Getting jilted at the altar did that to a woman.

Soon, all four of us were eating a delicious lunch and enjoying wonderful company. Everyone I cared about was around the white dinette table with me.

My cell phone rang. Recognizing Ted's number, I answered, "Hello?"

"Shelby, Lloyd just died. He was poisoned."

2

I glanced at the group around me. "Lloyd died of poisoning."

"From Joyce's cooking?" Grandma set down her glass. "I bet that was it."

I shook my head and turned by attention back to Ted. "What kind?"

"They won't know until they do an autopsy, but it was definitely something he ate."

I was not eating in the dining room again until Shady Acres had a new chef. "Keep us posted. Thank you for calling."

Grandma waved her fork at me. "You have to solve this, Shelby. It's an injustice."

"I seriously doubt the man was murdered…on purpose." I resumed my seat at the table.

Heath rubbed my back. His touch put me instantly at ease. "Perhaps the four of us should take turns cooking meals in our cottages?"

"Yes." Mom nodded. "Let's go grocery shopping after work."

"What about the rest of the residents? I need to let Alice know." We couldn't let the others potentially suffer as Lloyd did. I quickly ate my omelet, kissed Heath, something I never got enough of, and headed for the manager's office.

I searched for half an hour before I located Alice in the kitchen. She clutched a clipboard as a shield between her and Joyce and peered into a large pot. Two younger women, both kitchen helpers, busied themselves as far away from the chef as possible.

"What is it?" Alice asked, wrinkling her nose.

"Cabbage soup."

I wasn't going to try a single spoonful. "May I speak with you for a moment, Alice?"

"Can it wait? We're…discussing the supper menu."

"Not really." I motioned my head toward the door wanting to avoid the smell of that evening's meal.

"Fine." She sighed and followed me out the door, closing it behind her. "What?"

"Lloyd Dane is dead. Poisoned. From that woman's food." I pointed to the kitchen.

"Are you certain?"

"Not one hundred percent until the autopsy is done, but it's likely."

"Then please do not speculate." Alice narrowed her eyes. "I know Joyce is a horrible cook, but we signed a contract. I can't void it."

"No one is eating in the dining room anymore. How am I supposed to plan any kind of social when the food will be practically uneatable?"

"Let me see what I can do." She pushed back through the door into the kitchen, releasing a vocal argument between Joyce and her help.

I followed, despite the odor of the soup.

"You can't cook worth anything!" A tall, skinny brunette faced Joyce with a hard glint in her eyes. "You might as well poison us all and be done with it. You can't put that much salt in food for old people. Think of their blood pressure."

A plumb blond next to her nodded.

"There's a reason I'm the chef and you're the help." Joyce threw a wooden spoon at the brunette, who deftly ducked. "One more act of insubordination and I'll fire the both of you."

Alice cleared her throat. "I'm the only one capable of firing around here."

Joyce whirled, cursed, and stomped into the pantry. I had the irresistible urge to lock her in. Where in the world did Alice find such a person?

"Did you need something else, Shelby?" Alice asked.

I shook my head.

"Then, I'm certain you have work to do. I'm not paying you to stand around."

I shrugged and left, heading back to my golf cart to finish my rounds. After almost a year of working at Shady Acres, I was used to Alice's superior attitude, knew the stress she was under, and didn't take it personally.

No one was in Grandma's cottage, so I climbed onto the driver's seat of the cart and headed for the far boundary of the community. Flowers bloomed along flagstone walkways and around homes. Evergreen shrubs were trimmed. I still wanted to try my hand at turning the bushes into animal shapes. The koi pond sparkled. Shady Acres was a beautiful place to live despite the murders of the past.

With one hundred units, counting cottages and apartments, coming up with weekly social events was going to be a huge challenge. Perhaps I needed to convince Alice that a monthly get together was better now that we were growing. Still a challenge without a good chef.

I stopped in front of the maze…the place of so much fun and, yes, terror, in the past. Spotting poisonous mushrooms growing in the shade, I slid from the cart and dug them up, tossing them in a bin I kept behind the seat. I wouldn't want a senile resident to wander across them.

I'd just turned around when I spotted poison hemlock. Where was this stuff coming from? Sure, we'd had a lot of rain lately, but I cleared all undesirable plants from the grounds months ago. I dug it up and added it to the mushrooms. Talk about a deadly salad.

Wait. I dug my cell phone from my pocket and dialed Ted. "Have the poison people check for hemlock or mushrooms."

"Poison people?"

"You know. The ones doing the autopsy."

"Medical examiner." He sighed. "We'll be looking for several things."

"I also think you should get a warrant to search the kitchen here. Just in case Lloyd was intentionally poisoned."

"On what grounds?"

"I found poisonous plants."

"In the kitchen?"

"No." I groaned. "Outside."

"Don't look for false play where none exists." Click.

I guess that meant no warrant. Something niggled at my gut. An instinct I'd learned not to ignore. Something was once again shady in Shady Acres.

Resuming my seat in the cart, I swore not to get involved. If, and it was a big if, there was actually something to get involved in. I'd almost died twice. That was two times too many. I had to keep Grandma from thinking Lloyd might have died at the hands of a murderer. She'd nag me until I gave in and got involved.

Alice was right. I was bad luck to this place. Once a sleepy little community, a bit rundown, was now repaired, beautiful, and cursed.

When the supper bell rang, I declined eating at Mom's and chose to take my chances with the buffet. I surveyed the meager offerings, choosing fruit and cheese, which seemed safe. I carried my plate and a glass of sweet tea to a table.

It didn't take long for Heath to join me, a plate of his own with pizza. "I ordered." He handed me a slice. "What gives, gorgeous?"

"I can't shake the feeling that Lloyd wasn't accidentally poisoned." I told him about finding the poisonous plants. "Normally, I'd think these things grew naturally. Seeds dropped by birds, maybe. But the ground around them was freshly dug."

"You think Joyce poisoned him?" Heath sat back

in his chair. "That's a long stretch, her being the chef and all. She's the first person the authorities would look at."

"Then it has to be someone else in the kitchen. Who are the two helpers?"

"You really need to make an effort to meet everyone."

"I don't have time." I took a bite of melted cheese and pepperoni. Delicious.

"The tall brunette is Susan Hall. The blond is Lori Brown." He grinned and leaned his elbows on the table. "The person renting apartment 101 is Dean Roof. 103 is Madeline Cross. Those are the only new tenants so far."

I wasn't naïve enough to think that only a new resident was a killer. Any of the others could murder under the right circumstances. Wasn't that true of anyone?

"Stop looking for trouble," Heath said, plopping another pizza slice on my plate.

"You sound like Ted."

"You should listen."

"I'm only going to keep my eyes open." I finished off the pizza and stood. I almost told him I was going to search the kitchen after dark, but held my tongue. He'd either try to stop me or go with me. Since all I had to go on was a hunch, I'd go alone. If I found out there really was foul play, then I'd seek his help.

"I need to figure out what event to hold this weekend. It's so hot, I'm thinking a pool party. Black lights, rave music, all that sort of thing."

"These old folks might not like rave music."

I shrugged. "Maybe not, but why not broaden their horizons? They'll definitely like the black lights and white decorations." Maybe I'd rent a fog machine. "Anyway, I'm heading to my cottage to make up the fliers. See you at breakfast?"

"I'll be at your place to make pancakes by seven." He winked. "Just for the two of us."

I grinned. "That's a reason to wake up in the morning." After glancing around to make sure Alice wasn't within sight, I gave Heath a quick kiss. No sense rubbing salt in the wound of him choosing me over her. "See you then."

Back in my private space, I propped my bare feet on the coffee table and rested my laptop in my lap. My fliers tended to short, sweet, with lack of flourish, but they did the job. Every event was usually packed with residents.

I spent five minutes typing it, then printed it out. I'd get Alice's initials on it first thing in the morning, then have Mom put them in everyone's mailboxes. Last chore of the day complete, I decided a bit of research was called for.

A few minutes spent on a poison website and typed in Lloyd's symptoms. The names of several plants came up, including Fool's Parsley and Hemlock. Hmmm. Very interesting.

I glanced out my window. Heath was correct in the fact that Joyce shouldn't be considered the primary suspect right off the bat. After all...if someone were growing the poison on the grounds, it could be anyone. Since I tended to not always be the most observant person on the planet, they might think I wouldn't discover the plants.

I sent a text to Ted, letting him know of my discovery and got a knock on my door within five minutes. The man was nothing if not predictable.

"Hello, Ted," I said, whipping open the door.

"How did you know it was me?"

I gave him a look. "Seriously?"

He shook his head and pushed past me. "The autopsy is finished. I called in a favor and put in a rush job. Lloyd was poisoned by a leafy green plant, most likely. His stomach was full of it."

"One of the ones I texted you about?"

"The ME doesn't know yet. That might take a little longer."

I twisted my lips. "That doesn't give me a lot to go on."

"Stay of it," he growled.

I hadn't meant to say that out loud. "Something doesn't feel right, Ted. You know me and my instincts."

"That's what scares me. You got me shot and yourself almost killed a few months ago. I'm retired now. Let me live long enough to enjoy the days I have left." He turned and left, slamming the door behind him.

Alrighty then. I'd still learned something. Lloyd had been poisoned, and most likely by one of the plants grown right here. I planned on scouring the property tomorrow and pulling up anything that looked the least bit suspicious.

It wasn't like I was putting myself in danger, right? I was the gardener after all. What harm could come from pulling up weeds? But first, as soon as the sun set, I was visiting the kitchen.

3

Nine thirty p.m., and dressed in black yoga pants, a long sleeved black tee shirt, and a black beanie, I unlocked the door to the kitchen and stepped inside. I snapped on the flashlight headband and illuminated the space in front of me.

A spotless kitchen stood before me. A massive refrigerator took up half of one wall. A walk-in freezer the rest. Stainless steel countertops and appliances glistened in the light of my headlamp. Nothing looked out of place. Still, I wasn't giving up hope that I'd find a clue that would either convict Joyce or move my suspicion away from her.

I closed the door and headed for the garbage cans next to the door. I opened one and jerked back at the odor. The air filled with the sour smell of lots of wasted food. I didn't have the stomach to dig through it after all. I closed the lid and took deep breaths to settle my stomach.

Next, I headed for the refrigerator. At least the inside sported food ready to eat and nothing rotted. I opened the vegetable drawer and pulled out a leafy plant. One sniff told me I was looking at authentic parsley.

Just as I reached for a carton of orange juice, a thud sounded outside the kitchen door. I closed the fridge and ducked, turning off my headlamp. I didn't think the kitchen was off limits to me, I had a master key, after all, but I wasn't ashamed of admitting Joyce scared the piddle out of me. The last thing I wanted was for her to find me alone in her domain.

The kitchen door opened.

Whoever it was stepped inside the room.

I held my breath and clamped a hand over my mouth.

My heart thudded hard enough to be heard upstairs. Moving as slowly as possible, I crawled and peered around the corner of the island I'd hidden behind.

A dark figure opened a drawer. The moonlight through a high kitchen window glinted off a butcher knife.

I gasped and pulled back.

The overhead lights flickered on.

"Shelby?" Alice narrowed her eyes. "What in the world are you doing?"

"Maintenance?" I stood and wiped my hands down my thighs. "I heard there was a loose screw somewhere." No need to mention it's me.

"That is Heath's job, not yours." She headed for the door.

"Why the knife?" Like an idiot with no sense of

possible danger, I followed.

"I have a pest to get rid of." She pressed the button on the elevator. "You may come along if you wish."

I prayed she wasn't leading me into anything illegal or immoral and entered the elevator, standing as far away from her as possible.

She glanced at me, then shrugged. No doubt she was used to my weirdness. "This should actually be your job, not mine, but I can't get a wink of sleep until the deed is done."

Mercy.

The elevator stopped at the second floor, which was also the top floor. The doors opened and we stepped out. Alice led the way to her apartment. She had no number on her door, just a plague that read "Manager".

"Who are we going to kill?"

She narrowed her eyes. "Not who…what." She unlocked the door and stepped inside. "Shhh."

No problem.

"It's trapped in the bathroom."

"What is in there?" My hands shook.

"A rat."

"You're going to kill it with a knife?" My stomach rolled. "Why not trap it or set out poison? Call Heath!"

"I'm an independent woman, Shelby." She reached for the doorknob.

I swore I was never going out alone after dark again. Too many kooks in the dark. "I'm out of here. Don't come crying to me if you get bit." I dashed out of the room. There were two things I didn't deal with…snakes and rodents. Okay, three. I didn't do spiders either.

Not wanting to wait for the elevator, I dashed down the stairs. As I barged out the door, I ran smack dab into Heath's very muscular, very solid, very welcome chest.

"Whoa." He reached out to steady me. "What's the rush?"

I explained about Alice's lunacy and how I'd done nothing more than go into the kitchen to snoop when—

"That's why I'm here. I saw a light on in the kitchen. Now that I know it was you two, I'll head to Alice's apartment to take care of the rat."

"I'll head on home…" Was I nuts? He was headed to the apartment of a woman who liked him very much. At night, no less. "Nevermind. I'll come with you."

His sly grin told me he knew exactly why I'd changed my mind. The scoundrel. Still, I wasn't taking any chances.

A scream reverberated down the stairwell as Heath opened the door. A furry…thing streaked past our feet. I added my screams to Alice's and threw my arms around Heath's neck.

"Rat's gone," he said, laughing. "Good night, Alice."

"Good night!" The door at the top of the stairs slammed.

Heath walked me home, then left me with a kiss. It wasn't until I fell asleep that I realized I should have checked the outside dumpster. If anyone was going to throw away incriminating evidence, it wouldn't be inside.

~

Before the community woke, I had one leg over the lip of the dumpster trying to drum up the courage to jump inside. Because most everything was bagged, the smell wasn't quite as bad as the kitchen, but close enough to churn my stomach. Thankfully, I'd thought to bring a bandanna. I tied it around my nose and mouth and slid.

Bags stuffed full of only God knew what cushioned my fall. I sat for a moment, ears peeled for cries of alarm. When none came, I searched for poisonous plants. Ah ha! I reached for a sprig of parsley. One sniff told me it was the real thing used to garnish dinner plates.

I sat against a cardboard box. I was out of my mind. Lloyd had probably eaten something growing wild and poisoned himself accidentally. Why did I always assume something foul was going on?

A heavy bag fell on my head. Ow! I put one hand to my head while the other reached for the books spilling from the bag.

A Reader's Guide to Everyday Poisonous Plants. I struggled to my feet and peered over the edge of the dumpster. No one was in sight.

I shoved the book in the waistband of my shorts and tried hoisting myself out of the dumpster. Not as easy as getting in. On the outside I'd been able to pull up some cement blocks. Inside, everything shifted under my feet.

Finally, I threw one leg over.

A hand grabbed mine and pulled. I tumbled to the ground, landing at Ted's feet. "That was rude."

He scowled. "What are you doing in the dumpster?"

"Finding evidence." I handed him the book.

His eyes widened. He studied the book for a moment, then tucked it inside his shirt. "Your fingerprints are all over it. Stay out of this, Shelby." He turned to leave.

"Stay out of what?" I grabbed his arm. "There has to be something going on for me to stay out of."

"You stink. Go take a shower."

I sniffed. I definitely reeked. "This conversation isn't over, my friend." Not by a long shot. Ted knew something about Lloyd's death and I intended to find out what.

Ignoring the residents headed to breakfast, I hurried with my head down to my cottage. Shedding my clothes on the way to the bedroom, I tossed them in the hamper and turned on the shower spray.

Luckily, the only ones who'd spotted me during my failed attempts at sleuthing were Alice, Heath, and Ted. None of them would say anything, so I was safe…for the time being. Experience had taught me that wouldn't always be the case. If someone were behind Lloyd's death, they'd come after me the moment they discovered I was being nosy.

My thoughts raced as I stepped under the cool spray. I'd almost been convinced Lloyd's death was an unfortunate accident, then I'd found that book. I was building a case against…somebody.

4

A pounding on my front door greeted me as I stepped out of the shower. I wrapped a large towel around me and another around my hair and rushed to answer. Grandma stood there, her body quivering, and an earnest expression on her face. I stepped back and let her in.

"Where's your key?" I headed toward my bedroom.

"Forgot it." She bounded after me. "Teddy told me you were the dumpster. Who put you there?"

"I climbed in myself." I grabbed some clean clothes and went into the bathroom, closing the door behind me.

"Why would you…Oh! You were following a clue. What did you find?" Grandma said through the door.

"Give me a minute and I will tell you." I rolled my eyes and dropped my towel. Once I was dressed and my wild hair up in a messy bun, I joined Grandma in the living room. "I had a hunch—"

"No doubt. You get that from me." She handed me a cup of coffee.

"I think Lloyd was—"

"Poisoned. I know. Oh, you think he was murdered." Her eyes grew round.

"If you'd let me talk uninterrupted, I'll tell you what I think."

"Sorry." She sat at the glass-topped dinette table.

Eying her as if she were going to interrupt again, I sat across from her and told her everything that transpired, even Alice chasing the rat with a butcher knife.

When I'd finished, she stared into her coffee. "A rat, poison, and a dead man. Sounds like the title to a novel. So, Ted took the book you found? That means he agrees with you whether he admits it or not."

"My sentiments exactly."

"Now what?" she glanced up.

"I keep gathering information and turn it over to the authorities."

"Put yourself in danger again, you mean."

"Possibly."

She grinned. "Good. It's been months since there's been any excitement around here. Your mother is going to have a fit."

And Grandma derived great joy from that fact. "I'll be low key. My luck is bound to run out sometime." A tingle ran down my spine.

"Nah." Grandma waved her hand. "We're invincible." She stood. "I'm sure Sue Ellen has breakfast ready. It's pancakes."

That's all I needed to hear. My stomach rumbled all the way to Mom's cottage.

The moment I opened the door, the aroma of butter and syrup greeted me. Under that, I detected the woodsy cologne Heath wore. My morning was complete.

"We have another case to solve," Grandma announced, arms wide. "Uh-oh."

I peered around her into Ted's scowling face. "I know…stay out of it." I bent and gave Heath a kiss. "Good morning."

"Good morning." His husky voice and the darkening of his eyes made me want to kiss him longer and harder. But, with an audience, I'd have to take a raincheck. Still, since the food wasn't yet on the table, I perched in his lap and wrapped my arms around his neck.

"Busted," he whispered.

"Ted no longer has the authority to arrest me," I said, my lips close to his ear.

"No?" Ted crossed his arms. "I know plenty of officers who do have that authority."

"Teddy, darling," Grandma cooed, planting a scarlet kiss on his cheek. "Don't make threats you don't intend to follow up on."

"It's a promise, Ida."

I slipped off Heath's lap and helped Mom set out the food. Ted had been threatening to arrest me for getting in his way for months. It hadn't happened yet.

Mom gave a long-suffering sigh, but held her tongue. Poor thing. She knew how futile it was to stop Grandma and me when we were set on something.

I gave her a one-armed hug, my other hand holding

a syrup bottle. "We'll be careful. I promise."

"Don't you have enough work to do?"

"I can snoop while I'm working. All I need is to find out who is harvesting poisonous plants."

She sighed again. "Until you do, don't eat anything someone in this room didn't prepare."

"That's a definite." Two times over. Even then I might look twice at parsley or mushrooms.

5

"*W*hy do you not eat my food?" Joyce accosted me the moment I locked my cottage door the next morning.

"Oh! Uh…"

She poked me in the chest with her index finger. "You're too skinny. Come with me."

Feeling as if I were walking to my death, I shuffled along behind her to the kitchen. Once there, Joyce filled a plate with bacon and eggs and plopped it onto a small table. "Sit."

I nodded and complied. Where was a dog to feed scraps to when you needed one? How could I think such a thing? If the food were poisoned, I couldn't foist that on an unsuspecting animal.

"Eat!"

I shoved a mouthful of eggs into my mouth and chewed. Closing my eyes, I swallowed. When I didn't feel any symptoms after five bites, I relaxed and finished the food. "Wow, that was better than normal."

"Excuse me?" Joyce planted her fists on her ample hips.

"Oh. Sorry."

She whirled toward Susan. "You've been serving bad food? Must I do everything myself? Follow my instructions to the letter. I will now taste everything that is going to be served."

My eyes widened. Joyce hadn't been preparing the meals?

"I will give an apology," she said. "I will write a letter explaining the incompetence of my cooking help." She marched away.

I glanced up at Susan and Lori and shrugged. No sense in making more enemies. I picked up a slice of bacon. Just because Joyce wasn't the awful cook we all thought she was didn't mean she wasn't a killer. But, it did raise some doubts.

So, let's say Joyce isn't the culprit, intentionally or not. Lloyd's death could be the result of incompetence. But, if so, why had no one else taken sick? The only thing that made sense was that he was singled out by someone who knew their poison.

I set my plate in the large stainless steel sink, tossed a wave to the two helpers, and headed to work. As I stepped outside, Mom and Grandma marched toward me.

"We missed you at breakfast," Grandma said.

"Joyce fed me." I held up a hand to stop their protests. "Before you yell, I have to tell you she isn't the one that's been doing the cooking. The other two have and Joyce is very upset that the food hasn't been well-received."

"How do you feel?" Mom put a hand to my forehead.

"I'm fine. The bacon and eggs she fed me were quite good. I think the fare will improve."

"What about the poisoning?"

"I think Lloyd must have been an isolated incident. Maybe he ate the stuff himself." That was possible. Many residents harvested from the garden when they were in the mood to cook for themselves. The thing that plagued me, though, was how did poisonous plants get in the garden in the first place? That's the mystery I needed to solve.

"I'm happy," Mom said. "No more murder investigations to give me a heart attack."

"It's boring." Grandma sighed. "I'll go let Teddy know you're no longer going to be a thorn in his side." She marched toward the cottages while Mom headed to work at the reception desk.

I'd forgotten to give her the fliers to put in mailboxes. I hurried to my cottage and grabbed the stack from my table. Minutes later, I entered the foyer of the main building and stopped dead in my tracks.

A very handsome man around the age of sixty held my mother's hand to his lips. His blue eyes twinkled. "It's a pleasure to meet such a lovely gem as yourself," he said.

Mom giggled and slipped her hand free. "You're in apartment 101 Mr. Roof."

"I think I'll walk back out just so I can catch another glimpse of you as I stroll past."

I wanted to gag. "Here are the fliers, Mom." I gave the man a stern stare.

"You're a mother?" His lips twitched. "Why, I'd

take the two of you as sisters."

Seriously? "I need these handed out right away, please."

With another stern glance at Mr. Flirt, I turned and left. Mom wasn't going to date that man, was she? Was I ready for her to enter the dating pool? Dad had been gone for years. Yes, it was time. Mom deserved love, and it was time for me to stop being possessive. I'd have to apologize for behaving like a child.

I started to head back in when I caught sight of Lori Brown, a basket on her arm, head toward the herb section of the garden. I followed, ducking around bushes to stay out of sight.

She wandered the rows as if searching for something.

"May I help you?" I stepped out from behind a large hydrangea bush.

She gave a squeak, then nodded. "You scared me. I'm looking for the parsley."

"Have you tried the grocery store?"

"We had some the other day."

"You picked it yourself?"

"Of course. It's part of my job."

My blood chilled. "Lori, I don't grow parsley in this garden. What you picked was a poison."

Her mouth fell open, then she fainted right in the middle of my cucumber plants. I dug out my cell phone and called Ted.

He ran up about the time Lori was coming to. "Why don't you call the police? You know I'm retired."

"Force of habit. I think she accidentally poisoned Lloyd."

Lori covered her face with her hands. "He was

such a nice man. All I wanted to do was make his plate pretty." She peered up at me with red-rimmed eyes. "Who grows poison in a community garden?"

"That's what I want to know." I crossed my arms. "It sure wasn't me."

"Come with me, Miss Brown. The police will have some questions for you."

"Am I under arrest?" The tears flowed down her round cheeks.

"I'm sure you'll be home by supper." Ted escorted her out of sight.

I retrieved her basket and headed to the kitchen. Joyce would need to know she was temporarily minus a helper. Relief that Lloyd's death had truly been an accident flooded through me. The imbedding of the plants was still a mystery, but at least I wasn't dealing with a murderer. Just a horticultural idiot.

~

"Howdy." Heath wrapped his arms around my waist from behind and lifted me off my feet. "I heard Lloyd's death was an accident."

I slipped free and turned to face him. "It appears so."

His eyes narrowed. "You don't believe it?"

"No, I do, but I'm still curious as to where the plants came from."

He took my hand. "Let's sneak down to the creek and take a break. It's hot. You need to let go of the fact there's a mystery here."

He was right. I wiped the back of one gloved hand across my perspiring forehead. "A dip in the creek sounds like just what I need."

Heath hopped into the passenger side of my golf

cart and I drove us past the maze and into the trees. I stayed too busy to enjoy the fifty acres of wooded land that bordered the far end of the community. Some of the residents had mentioned how peaceful the walking trail was and how clear and cold the creek. I really did need to make time to relax more.

Parking in the shade of an oak tree, I slid from my seat and kicked off my rubber gardening boots. Yes, I could wear something cooler on my feet, like flip-flops, but I liked my boots. They were my trademark. I set my phone in the cart's cup holder and ran to the water.

I gasped at the water's frigidness as I stepped in the creek up to my ankle. Within seconds, my feet were deliciously numb. Before I could venture further, I found myself swept up in Heath's arms and dumped into a deep section.

The water stole my breath. I pushed both feet against the sandy bottom and popped up. "That was mean!" I sent an arc of water with both hands, catching him in the face.

"Don't you feel cooled off?" He laughed and ducked under. He grabbed my ankles and yanked.

I submerged again, and came up laughing. "We should play more often."

He snaked his arm around my waist and pulled me close. "Most of our alone time is spent finding killers and running for our lives. I agree this is much better."

"Hmm." I rested my cheek against his chest and listened to his heartbeat. "I thank God every day for you coming into my life." After being ditched at the altar last year, I didn't think I could find love again.

When our lips were blue and we were tired, we crawled up on the bank and lay down in a patch of leaves under the trees. I leaned on one elbow and studied Heath's profile, flicking a blond curl with one finger. "You look just like Chris Hemsworth."

"You mean Thor? I'll take it." A dimple winked in his cheek. "Except for the long hair. I don't think that would suit me."

I laughed and flopped onto my back. "We should head back. Someone will be looking for us."

"Alice is off the grounds. Something about a corporate meeting."

"Ah, so the cat's away and the mice will play?"

He rolled over on top of me. "Most definitely. Still cold?"

"A little." I wrapped my arms around his neck. "Want to warm me up?"

"Like this?" He nuzzled my ear. "Or this," he said, trailing kisses down my neck.

I shuddered and it had nothing to do with the cold water.

Heath proceeded to kiss me until I was dizzy, not stopping until my stomach growled. "I see how it is. With you, food always comes first." He stood.

"Most often. You're dessert, not the appetizer." I held out my hand so he could pull me to my feet.

I wiped away leaves that had dried to the back of my legs and rear end, then bent to pull on my boots. My gaze fell on a newly dug patch of dirt. I knelt next to the hole. A foot away was another one. In between the holes was a size eight and half foot print. I knew that because the print was the same size as the shoes I wore.

I'd found out where the plants in my garden came from. Now to match the show print. I retrieved my phone from the golf cart and snapped some pictures.

"What's up?" Heath peered over my shoulder.

"I think the poisonous plants came from here."

He ran his fingers through his hair. "Why are you still digging into this?"

"Because putting poisonous plants in my garden is dangerous. Someone died." I studied his face. "I want to find out who the culprit is and tell them that unless they know without a doubt what plants are safe, they shouldn't be digging them out of the forest. What if they die because of not knowing?"

6

"*G*ood job on improving the food around here."

I glanced from where I weeded the garden to see Alice, clutching her clipboard, standing over me. I pushed to my feet, groaning as my knees popped. "All I had to do was bring it to Joyce's attention."

Her face fell. "Sometimes I think you would make a better manager than me."

"Don't be silly. We both know this place would fold with me at the helm. I'm much too flighty." I patted her shoulder and gripped the handles of the wheelbarrow where I'd tossed the pulled weeds. Once my steel barrel was full, I'd burn them behind the shed.

"I feel like a hamster on a wheel." She trotted alongside me. "You've made the grounds something of beauty. I feel like I never reach the end of my to-do pile."

Okay. I stopped. Alice obviously needed some encouragement. "Maybe you need a vacation. It has been a stressful year."

"True. Murder and theft does take the starch out of a person. I'll consider it. Thank you. Now, back to work. Heath is almost finished painting the apartments and I need to fill them. Ciao!"

Sometimes I thought the woman only spoke to me so she could make sure I was working. I continued to my weed pile and scooped the weeds into the barrel. As I did, I noticed there seemed to be less of the poisonous ones there. I'd tossed them yesterday.

I glanced at the ground, noting the same size footprints as I'd seen near the creek. All thoughts of accident picking flew into the air. If someone wanted to take them from my trash heap, then they had done it on purpose.

Last summer, my best friend Cheryl Leroix had stayed with me for a few weeks of her summer break and helped me catch a killer. I needed her again. Pulling my cell phone from my pocket, I dialed her number.

"Hey girl." My Amazon-like friend's voice was soft and sultry. When she'd visited the first time, the old geezers had been all goo-goo ga-ga over her curves.

"What are you doing during your last three weeks of summer?"

"Got another mystery? I hated missing the one last fall. Try not to get involved unless I'm on break, okay?"

I laughed. "I'll do my best." I explained all that had transpired.

"Sounds intriguing. I'll pack a bag and be there by supper."

"Thank you. Bye." I hung up, relieved that Grandma wouldn't be my only sidekick. Cheryl was much more sensible when it came to staying out of trouble.

Finished weeding, I hopped in my golf cart and headed to the koi pond. A few months back, the decoration had held more than colorful fish and water foliage. I'd discovered a resident's body face down in the pond. This time, all was as it should be. I sat for a moment and let the peace surround me as I contemplated what I needed to do next.

Now that the complex was in pretty good order, I wasn't running from one task to the other worrying I wouldn't finish. I steered the golf cart toward my cottage. I'd wash the guest linens in preparation for my friend.

As I cleaned and did laundry, I thought on how I could find out who matched the footprints I'd found. It had to be a woman or a very small man. And, it had to be someone who had access to food, either in a private cottage or the public dining room. Which sent me right back to not wanting to eat at the buffet.

I called Grandma. "I have a job for you."

"As in sleuthing?"

"Yes. I need you to arrive at the buffet early enough to watch everything being put out and make sure nobody adds anything to the food."

"Sounds boring."

"Sometimes playing spy is boring. Will you do it?"

She sighed. "Of course. If I catch someone, I'll snap their picture and take the tray to Teddy so he can hand it over to forensics."

"Thank you, Grandma. You're the best."

"Well, don't tell anyone. I wouldn't want to lose my tough girl reputation." Click.

By the time the lunch bell rang, I'd completed my

chores at home and was more than ready to eat. I stepped into the dining room to chaos.

"I saw you sprinkling something in the salad!" Grandma tugged one end of the tray.

"It was Italian seasoning!" Birdie tugged on the other end. "You crazy old broad. You know me. What is wrong with you?"

"Shelby gave me a job to do, and I intend to it." Yank.

"Grandma. Birdie." I took the tray and set it back on the buffet table. "Birdie wouldn't poison anyone."

"I might poison *her*." She glared at Grandma.

So much for subtlety. "You're making a scene. Please fill your plates and go to your tables." I bent over the salad and sniffed. Smelled like Italian seasoning, but I'd pass.

"Why are you sniffing the salad?" Heath whispered in my ear.

Goosebumps pimpled my skin from his nearness. "I guess you missed the drama."

"No, I saw it. Quite amusing. Do you really think Birdie capable of harming anyone?"

"Not really. Plus, I think her feet are too small."

He chuckled. "Come on. Let's eat." As if to make a point, he filled his plate with salad. Heath never ate salad.

I chose a chicken salad sandwich and a fruit plate. Just to be safe.

While we ate, and Heath shoveled in big bites of salad into his grinning mouth, I watched him for signs of anything amiss. About half way through his plate, his eyes widened and he clutched his stomach.

I bolted out of my chair. "What is it? Oh, my

Lord."

He laughed. "Nothing. Just playing. The salad is delicious…if you like rabbit food."

I punched his arm. "Not funny." I plopped back in my seat and glared over my sandwich.

"I cannot believe you're eating that." Grandma sat next to Heath. "Didn't you see Birdie tampering with it?"

"Seasoning, Ida." Ted joined us, shaking his head. "Shelby, please don't assign your grandmother any more jobs."

"I won't have to. Cheryl will be here by supper." I took a big gulp of ice water.

"But I want to be involved." Grandma pouted.

"None of you should get involved. I'm talking to walls here." Ted tossed his napkin on the table.

"Settle down, dear. I'll be more careful to do my nosing around without you knowing." Grandma patted his hand.

He growled in his throat and bit into his hamburger.

Poor Ted. Maybe retiring where Grandma and I lived hadn't been the wisest choice he could have made. Now he was subject to our shenanigans before we called for help. He had a front row seat.

"The next time…the very next time…one of you butts into a police investigation, I will have you arrested." Ted stood and planted his hands flat on the table. "Mark my words." Then, he marched away, leaving us all with our mouths hanging open.

He'd threatened before, but this time I think he meant every word.

7

"*C*heryl!" I raced down the pathway and into the strong arms of my friend.

She rocked me back and forth, then set me at arm's length. "You look good. All tanned and fit. Gardening agrees with you."

"Thanks. I love it." I linked my arm with her's as we moseyed to my cottage. After putting her things in the guest room, we plopped on the sofa and faced each other.

"So, how's the good looking handyman?" she asked.

"Quite well, thank you." My face heated and my grin spread.

"No commitment?"

I shook my head. "I'm not ready for that. A few months ago, an ex of his turned up."

"I read about her in the newspaper. Crazy woman.

That doesn't mean you have anything to worry about with Heath. He's solid."

"My heart knows that, but my head keeps reminding me of my…wedding failure." I took a deep breath. "Change of subject. Any ideas on how to find out who's been harvesting the forest of poisonous plants?"

"Not a clue." She crossed her ankles and propped them on the coffee table. "I guess we study shoes at supper and pay attention to who comes and goes on the walking trails. I feel like Nancy Drew and Beth."

I laughed. "Only Nancy always had a plan. I feel like I have to stumble across the clues."

The supper bell rang and we both jumped to our feet.

"Let's get this party started." Cheryl grinned and opened the front door. "Remember…look at the feet."

"Got it, boss." I saluted and stepped out, locking the cottage door behind us.

Conversation stopped and old men's eyes bugged when Cheryl entered the diningroom. "I've missed the adoration," she said, smiling. "Third graders love me but they don't look at me as if I'm prime rib."

"I should hope not." I grinned across the room at Heath and headed for the buffet. Oh, right, shoes.

I glanced down at the shoes of those in line with me. Of course, now that Cheryl was there, men crowded the line, all wanting to be the one to fill her plate. It made it difficult to find size eight-and-a-halfs in the throng. I needed a plan.

After filling my plate with roast beef and mashed potatoes, I joined Heath and my family at our usual table. It took a while for Cheryl to get free, her plate piled with more food than one person could possibly eat, and sit with us.

"Wow. Just wow." She sat and released a heavy breath. "Viagra must run rampant in this place."

"It's just that you aren't what they see every day." Mom patted her hand. "No vulgarity at the table, please."

Cheryl raised her eyebrows in my direction. I shrugged and turned my attention to my food, hoping it tasted as good as it looked.

"Shelby?" Alice tottered on stilettos toward me.

Why would anyone want to wear such torture devices all day? "Yep, that's me."

She frowned. "A word in private, please."

I shrugged, glanced around the table, then grabbed a roll off Cheryl's plate and followed Alice to her office. "What's up? Couldn't it wait until after supper?"

"Not really." She pointed to a plant lying on a paper towel on top of her desk. "I found that growing in a pot behind Heath's workshop. I think it's marijuana."

"You're right." I grinned. Some old geezer was mellowing out in the evenings. I suppose it could be for medicinal purposes, but I liked my first theory better.

"Do you think it's Heath's?"

My smile faded. "Of course not." Seriously? What about Heath could lead her to suspect such a possibility? Heath was good, kind, upstanding…I realized she was still talking.

"—asleep in the middle of the day, and—"

"Who was asleep in the middle of the day?"

"Heath. Pay attention, Shelby. I've heard pot makes you sleepy."

"I'm sure there's a reasonable explanation. Have

you asked him?"

"No. What if he gets angry?"

"Angry? Are we talking about the same man?" Heath never got more than irritated. "I'll ask him for you, how's that?"

"Oh, thank you." She clasped her hands together. "Now, get rid of that, please."

"Oh, good grief." The woman was helpless. I scooped up the bit of plant and paper towel and dumped both in the first trashcan I came across after entering the dining room.

"What did she want?" Heath glanced up.

"She wanted to know why there is marijuana growing behind your work shop." I sat down.

"There is?" Grandma clapped her hands. "I hope you'll share."

Ted put his hands over hers. "It's illegal, Ida. So, Heath, what do you have to say or yourself?"

"It's not mine." He forked a bit of roast into his mouth. "I'm sure someone with glaucoma is growing it."

Ted narrowed his eyes. "Then why not in their cottage?"

Heath set his fork down with a clank. "Do you honestly think if I were doing something illegal that I would do it right out in front of God and everybody? There are acres of woods out there for that sort of thing."

I watched the exchange with crossed arms. Could someone be trying to frame Heath as they had tried doing once before? A handyman, with access to everywhere in Shady Acres, would be the easiest to try and pin something on. They'd failed then, why try again?

Cheryl leaned close and whispered, "I bet if Alice would have checked for prints, she would have found size eight and a half?"

I nodded. "My thoughts exactly. Someone knows their plants. Now, to find out who."

"Shelby, I'm warning you to—" Teddy glared.

"I know, stay out of it or you'll lock me up. Old story, same paragraph." I quickly finished eating, whispered to Heath not to worry, no one believes him capable of doing anything illegal, then motioned for Cheryl to follow me.

"Got a light?" I asked.

"On my phone."

"Good. Let's go investigate behind the work shop once it's dark."

"What are we going to do now?"

"Search the maze for poisonous plants until it's too dark."

Cheryl stopped. "I'm not going in there. Are you crazy? Have you forgotten what happened a few months ago?"

"We had a wonderful party after all that happened. It's not dangerous. Stop being an Amazon baby."

"Mentioning my size is plain mean." She stormed ahead of me down the pathway.

Always sensitive about her height. My friend wasn't fat in any sense of the word, but she was five feet ten inches tall, big-boned and big chested, with a mane of blond hair that curled down her back. Men ogled and women stared. She was a true beauty. I knew mentioning her size would get her moving.

She stopped at the entrance to the maze. "You first.

I don't know my way around."

"Okay. Keep your eyes open for parsley, mushrooms, or marijuana."

She rolled her eyes. "I don't know what anything but the mushrooms look like."

"Then just keep me company." Despite my brave front, the maze scared me after dark. But, if a person didn't want anyone guessing what you were up to, the cover of darkness was the safest way.

We made it all the way to the gazebo in the center without finding a thing out of place. I sat on one of the benches. "I guess no one thought of doing anything illegal here."

Cheryl sat beside me. "Do the old folks actually stroll through here?"

"All the time." I wiggled my eyebrows. "It's where they have their secret rendezvous."

"Gross." She squared her shoulders. "It's lovely. Can we go now? By the time we get back, it'll be dark enough to go behind the work shop."

I nodded and led the way.

With the sun setting, a few residents wandered the grounds. Some liked to stroll the gardens after supper, but most settled down in their cottages to watch their favorite programs and get ready for bed. Unless we had a social function. At that time, they all showed up.

We turned the corner of the work shop. Grandma leaned against the wall. "I knew you'd come. Didn't think it would take this long, though."

"How long have you been here?" I should have brought water. The walk through the maze was long and the evening was still warm. I fanned myself with my hand.

"Since shortly after supper." She leaned and peered into my face. "Now tell me why you broke my heart snooping around without me. Has Cheryl taken my place as your partner?"

"Never." I kissed her cheek. "But, you're always with Ted."

"No one can replace you, Ida." Cheryl wrapped her in a hug. "Now, tell me you haven't trampled over any footprints."

"I'm not an idiot. The plant is over there. Alice only snipped off part of it." She held out her phone. "I've taken photos."

"Good job!" I directed Cheryl to shine her light in that direction. Sure enough. Size eight and a half prints were next to the plant. With my phone, I snapped a few more photos. "Ted can take over now."

"Good to know." He came around the corner with a police officer who stood so rigid, I would have sworn he had an iron rod for a spine. "This is Office Willis. He'll take over from here."

I stepped back and glanced at Cheryl. With wide eyes and open mouth, she stared at the officer. I suppose she might think the man handsome. He stood a few inches taller than her, a rarity, and had dark hair cut in a buzz cut. Dark eyes glittered in the light of our phones.

"Uh, nice to meet you." I held out my hand.

He nodded, not returning my shake. "Mr. Lawrence has warned me about you three."

"I'm sure he has." I grinned. "But, you'll grow to love us."

"I doubt it." He squatted next to the bush. "Who's the gardener here?"

"I am."

"I'll be taking you to the station for questioning."
He pulled a pair of handcuffs from his belt.

8

"I've done nothing against the law." I pulled back, hiding my hands behind me.

How dare Ted bring some rookie to arrest me for doing my job? As gardener, it was my responsibility to care for *all* plants on the grounds.

"We can do this the easy way or the hard way," Officer Willis said.

Heath took a step forward, only to have his way blocked by Ted. Heath scowled and kept his gaze on me over Ted's shoulder. "I'll bail you out," he mouthed.

"Teddy!" Grandma put her hands on her hips. "What in heaven's name are you doing?"

"Arresting two troublemakers."

"Two? Oh." She eyed the other set of cuffs hanging on Office Willis's belt, then turned and ran as fast as a sixty-something-year-old woman could run.

"Don't add fleeing arrest to your charges, ma'am," Officer Willis called. He snapped the cuffs on me. "Stay here."

It didn't take many steps with his long legs long for him to catch up to Grandma. A few seconds later, he dragged a squirming woman to my side. "Mr. Lawrence, your help in getting these two to my patrol car would be appreciated."

Cheryl narrowed her eyes. "You know," she wiggled her fingers between him and her, "I almost thought there could maybe be something between you and I. How wrong could I be?"

"Just doing my job, ma'am." He took me by the elbow, leaving Ted to take an irate Grandma, and led me down the walkway to the parking lot.

He opened the back door. "Watch your head." He helped me inside and closed the door while Ted did the same on the other side with Grandma.

"We are finished, Theodore Lawrence," she said. "Do you hear me? Finished."

"Okay, sweetie." He closed the door.

"I don't think he believes you," I said, glaring at the back of Office Willis's head. Seriously, all the times I'd actually interfered in an investigation and this is the time they chose to lock me up?

"Russian roulette," I muttered.

"What's that?" Grandma peered into my face.

"It was only a matter of time." I faced her. "It's an addiction. I can't help myself."

"Stop talking. Anything you say can—hey! You didn't read us our rights." She kicked the back of the seat.

Willis ignored her until the third kick. "You are

starting to get on my nerves, ma'am."

"Ugh." She flounced back in the seat.

"Behave. You're making things worse." I sighed and glanced out the window at the night.

A dark figure stood on the side of the road as we pulled out of the parking lot. He, or she, lifted their hand in a wave, then strolled behind the building. I think I'd just gotten my first look at a very happy murderer who wanted me out of the way, even if for only a short time.

"Turn around! Pull over. I'm going to be sick." I had to get out of the car.

Officer Willis pulled to the side of the road and hurriedly opened the door. "Don't get any in the car." He gagged and turned away. I'd find the giant's weakness.

I took off running toward Shady Acres. Not an easy feat with my hands tied behind me.

"Hey!" Willis caught me in short order. "You two are giving me gray hairs."

"I think I saw the murderer. You have to go after them."

"What murderer?"

I motioned with my head. "The one who poisoned Lloyd Dane. Seriously? Why do you think you're hauling me away? Because you think I grew poisonous plants and put them in his food, right?"

He crossed his arms. "No. You're here because you're growing marijuana. Allegedly. I think you need to explain a bit more about the poison."

"The person is getting away." Ugh. Why did no one in law enforcement ever believe me until I was facing down a killer? "Whatever. Take me to the station." I marched back to the car. I'd be out in no time. He hadn't read us our rights and had no proof I'd planted the marijuana. Someone told a tall tale and I intended to find out whom.

Grandma started squawking again the moment Officer Willis stopped in front of the precinct. "It's past my bedtime. I didn't have my medicinal wine. You've got nothing on us."

I groaned and slid from the backseat once he opened the door. "Hush, Grandma. We'll be home soon."

Officer Willis led us to a small room where they took our fingerprints and mugshots. Completely unfair. My hair was a mess and I looked horrible in black.

Grandma grinned like she was having a glamour shot taken.

Once that torture was over, Grandma was locked in a holding cell and Officer Willis escorted me to an interrogation room. It sounded fancier than it was. Actually, it was nothing more than a closet-sized room with a table and a chair on each side. I didn't even warrant a two-way mirror.

"Sit." Officer Willis motioned me to one of the chairs. "Tell me about the plant behind the woodshed."

"The manager, Alice Johnson, brought me a twig of the plant and told me where she'd gotten it." I stared at a stain on the wall behind his head that looked remarkably like the state of Texas. The stain, not his head.

"Where is that twig now?"

"I threw it in the diningroom trashcan, so I'm assuming it's in the dumpster." I leaned forward. "Look. You're wasting your time and mine. I didn't plant the marijuana. I've found poison hemlock and mushrooms in my herb garden and along the hiking trails. Someone is growing the stuff, on purpose or accidently, I haven't yet determined. Is it against the law for me to want to know who is messing with my garden?" There. That sounded as if I really knew my stuff. I sat back with a satisfied grin.

Officer Willis stared impassively at me, then gave a tiny shake of his head. "We got an anonymous phone call about you growing marijuana. I pull up and there you are. I'm new to the precinct. A week actually. I didn't know about the Dane case or that it was even still open."

"You believe me?" Finally. I heaved a long sigh.

"Not necessarily, but I will look into the plants." He stood and pulled a handcuff key from his pocket.

"You're letting me go?"

"You're only here as a favor to Ted. He's my uncle. He wanted to teach you a lesson. I don't think it worked."

"Not at all." Boy, was I going to have a word with Ted! "That makes you and Alice cousins...or are you her brother?"

He smiled. "Cousins. Let's go spring your grandmother." He unlocked the cuffs.

We heard Grandma long before we saw her. Slightly off-key, she sang, "Nobody knows the trouble I've seen. Nobody knows—" She dashed to the bars of her cell. "My turn?"

"You're free to go, Mrs. Grayson."

"Free! How long was I in the slammer? It seemed like forever. Is it morning yet?"

I rolled my eyes. "Less than thirty minutes,

Grandma. Stop being dramatic." I put my arm around her shoulders. "The nice Mr. Willis is going to give us a ride home. Aren't you, Officer?"

"Uh, yeah. I want to meet that tall friend of yours."

I laughed. "She might hit you, but I'll make the introduction." In fact, after his and Ted's little game to try and teach Grandma and me a lesson, I'd like to see my friend clobber him.

~

When we arrived at Shady Acres, Grandma headed for Ted's cottage with steam coming from her ears. Despite the late hour, the feisty old woman marched on heels high enough to bring down a younger woman. I almost felt sorry for the retired police officer.

I unlocked the door to my cottage and stepped inside. Cheryl sat on the couch idly flipping through channels on the television.

"That was fast." She pressed the off button on the remote. "Did that jerk realize you aren't one of the bad guys?"

"I did." Officer Willis stepped followed me through the door and approached Cheryl with hand extended. "I'm Seth Willis. It's a privilege to meet you."

"Hmmph." Cheryl stuck her nose in the air.

"I told you." I headed for the kitchen for a glass of water.

I chuckled listening to Officer Willis try and make small talk with Cheryl. She answered in monosyllables. Still, I recognized the light of interest in her eyes. She was only playing hard to get. The poor man had no idea what he was in for.

I carried a pitcher filled with ice water and three

glasses to the coffee table. "I explained to Officer Willis about the plants I've found. Taking me to the station was only a ploy on Ted's part to keep me from nosing around."

"That's a sick joke. I was worried." Cheryl glared at Officer Willis.

"Please. When I'm off duty, call me Seth."

"You're still in uniform," I said, pouring him a glass. "I have a question for you."

"Shoot." He grinned and accepted the water.

"What's my next move? It's obvious someone is trying to set me up." I handed Cheryl a full glass, poured one of my own, and then sat on the sofa next to my friend.

He grew serious. "Don't go anywhere alone. All any of the other officers could talk about my first day here was the previous murders that occurred here in Boonesville. Which you were involved in. Homicide isn't a game, Shelby."

"I know that, but I've a knack for seeing things the authorities don't." That...and the luck of being in the right place at the right time.

Heath burst in the front door.

Officer Willis stood, pulling his weapon from its holster.

Heath skid to a stop and put his hands up. "I'm friendly." He glanced over at me.

"Not smart barging in like that." Officer Willis put his gun away and sat back down.

"I heard Shelby was back." He pulled me into his arms. "Are you okay?"

"I'm fine. Just a prank."

"I know. Ida told me, sort of. I could hear her

screaming two cottages down. Ted is getting quite the tear down." A corner of his mouth curved. He turned and offered a handshake to Office Willis. "Heath McLeroy. Future fiancé."

I giggled. He hadn't proposed, yet, but it was obvious he saw the tall officer as a threat.

"I'm interested in the other gal." Officer Willis returned his shake. "I like them hardy. No offense, Shelby, but you look like a strong wind could carry you away."

Heath shook his hand, then pulled me down on the sofa next to him. "She's stronger than she looks."

"Back up," Cheryl said. "You're actually interested in me?"

"Yes." He grinned. "I think I might have met my match in being hard-headed with you. I look forward to the challenge."

Her cheeks reddened. "We'll see. Goodnight all." Ducking her head to try and hide a grin, Cheryl headed down the hallway.

"I'll be back tomorrow," Officer Willis said. "I'd like to take a look at the spot you found the other plants."

After he left, Heath and I snuggled on the sofa a bit before I started going cross-eyed and yawning more than I was kissing. I stood and tugged him up. "I love you. See you in…" I glanced at the clock. "Six hours."

He tapped my nose with his finger. "I'll be going with you and Officer tall, dark, and handsome in the morning."

I smiled. "I wouldn't want it any other way." I saw him to the door, locking it behind him.

I actually felt a bit of hope in Office Willis

showing interest in the case. It wasn't common for the authorities to believe anything I said. Until bullets started flying. Then, they believed sure enough.

9

*O*fficer Willis hadn't shown up by breakfast, so I joined the usual crowd at the usual table and ate the usual food. I loved my job and where I lived, but if not for the occasional mystery to liven things up, I feared I'd grow bored. What a hobby I'd chosen.

"Uh-oh, here comes the chef," Mom whispered. "She looks mad."

"Come." She crooked a finger at me.

I glanced around the table, glared at Ted, who shrugged, then got up and followed Joyce to the kitchen. "What's wrong?"

"Keep your mouth shut about this. I don't want suspicion turned on me." Joyce led me to the large walk-in pantry. "The cops are up my skirt enough as it is." She grabbed some parsley. "Smell that."

I sniffed. "So?"

"Not parsley." She shoved it into my hands. "Take it to your cop friend. You know what it is. You're a gardener."

I did know it was poison hemlock I held in my bare hands. Could it seep through my skin? Was this her plan all along? To get rid of me?

"They'll want to know where I got it." Which would point directly to Joyce as the primary suspect. Was she a murderer? I noticed the hard glint in her eyes. Was this a ploy to throw the authorities off her scent? "Is it possible one of your helpers picked the wrong plant?"

"Anything is possible with those two. Dumber than a stump." She gave me a nudge toward the door. "Go. Take that away."

I glanced around for her helpers before leaving. Why were those two so rarely seen?

"What's that?" Office Willis stepped around the corner. "More poisonous plants?"

"Don't look at me like that. I thought we reached an agreement last night." I dumped the plants in the garbage. "Be right back." I couldn't get into the women's restroom fast enough to wash my hands. After washing them enough times to turn the skin wrinkly, I returned to the scowling Office Willis. "You're much nicer when you're off duty."

"Every time poison shows up, there you are."

"It's an illness. Ask Ted. Now, I'm going to go finish my breakfast…you're welcome to join us…then, I'll take you to the woods."

He grinned. "Sounds like my father when he was going to spank me."

My mouth fell open. Was he flirting with me? Mercy. Cheryl would kill me first and him second. I snapped my mouth closed and marched to the table.

Cheryl straightened.

Grandma glared.

Heath glowered.

Mom glanced up, most likely wondering why a police officer was escorting me.

"Sit." I pointed to an empty seat next to Cheryl and took mine beside Heath. "I'll explain later," I told them.

While I ate my ham and cheese omelet, fresh and warm, thanks to Heath who must have gotten me a new plate, I pondered the predicament of the poisonous plants. Who in Shady Acres would know the difference? Surely thinking it was accidental picking was foolish.

I knew the difference, so did Joyce. Heath, too. Two of these names were not the killer. I needed to find out whether the kitchen help, Susan and Lori, had experience with plants. Then, there were the guests. The usual crowd didn't seem likely. That left the newbies, Dean Roof and Madeline Cross. I needed to find out more about them.

I was so deep in my thoughts it took a moment to realize Officer Willis was telling the others about me leaving the kitchen with the hemlock. "She was clutching it like a bouquet of roses."

"Sometimes I wonder what's in her head," Ted said.

"Excuse me? I'm sitting right here." I set my tea glass down with a thunk. "I took the plants from Joyce." Ooops. Promise already broken.

Both men's eyes narrowed. "What was she doing

with them?" Officer Willis asked.

"She said she found them in her pantry and for me not to say anything." Great. I'd said too much again.

As if one, they stood and marched for the kitchen.

I sighed and figured the best course of action was to leave. I jumped up and dashed out the door like a coward. I couldn't bear to look into Joyce's face when they hauled her out.

I headed for my tool shed and waited in the golf cart. Officer Willis could come and find me.

It didn't take long. About fifteen minutes later, he and Heath climbed into the cart.

"What happened?" I peered into Officer Willis's face.

"She broke down into tears, believe it or not." He shook his head. "Since we've no more evidence than your word, we can't hold her."

Wonderful. She was hurt and mad at me. She sure didn't seem like the crying type. Not to mention that, if she were a murderer, I'd just put a target on my back.

"You're normally a chatterbox," Officer Willis stated.

"I'm not telling you anything about anyone ever again."

"You have to." He glanced in the backseat at Heath. "Tell her."

"You can't withhold evidence," Heath said.

"I know that. But I didn't have evidence. I had speculation." I sent us down the walkway at a ripping ten miles per hour.

I drove to where Heath and I had found the plants near the creek. "I'll stay here, out of the way…Seth."

"Uh-oh," Heath said. "She isn't respecting the

uniform."

Seth shrugged and knelt next to where the plants had been. "Have you made a list of those who wear eight and half?"

"I was going to, but then you hauled me to jail. I'll try to do it at lunch." I held up my foot. "All I have to do is compare their foot to mine."

He straightened. "You do realize all the evidence points to you, right?"

"I suppose that means you'll be keeping an eye on me, just in case." Too bad the evidence didn't point to Cheryl. She's the one who wanted his attention. I already had a man.

Seth snapped some pictures and climbed back in the cart. He turned and faced me. "Who are your suspects? Ted said you always have a list."

"I haven't had time to make one."

"Maybe not on paper, but..." he tapped my head with his finger, "I'm sure you have one up there. Suspects and reasons, please."

"Joyce, for obvious reasons. Her helpers...for the same reasons. That's about it. I intend to find out who knows about horticulture."

"How do you intend to that?"

I shrugged. "No idea, yet. Aren't you going to tell me to stay out of things?"

He laughed. "The precinct has a file on you, Shelby Hart. You're an asset. But...that doesn't mean you aren't capable of murder."

"I don't have a motive."

"I hope I don't find one."

Heath was awfully quiet in the backseat. I turned. "What's on your mind?"

"I think Seth needs to dig into the victim's life and see whether there is a connection to you. If not, he can stop looking at you as a suspect and move on to someone else."

"Good idea!" I grinned and raised my eyebrows at Seth.

"I'm already doing that." He crossed his arms and stared straight ahead. "Let's hope I don't find anything."

~

I headed for the dining hall only to discover a sign on the door that said no service for Shelby Hart. Since I didn't think Joyce could actually refuse me food, I entered. She'd made her point very clearly. I needed to apologize.

"Get out!" She waved a gravy laden spoon at me the moment I entered the kitchen.

"I came to apologize. It just slipped out. They were making fun of me for caring the plants and—"

"I don't care. Now they think I'm a murderer."

I glanced at her feet. "What size shoe do you wear?"

"Eight and a half. Why?"

"Just wondering." I turned to the kitchen help. "What about you two?"

Susan glanced at the ugly, white non-skid shoes on her feet. "Eight and a half. I have small feet for a woman of my height."

Lori, eyes wide, glanced around the room. "I wear a size six."

"Thank you." I marched out of the kitchen. "Two suspects," I muttered.

The kitchen door slammed behind me.

I turned to see Susan glaring at me as she headed down the hall. Great. Make that two suspects who didn't like me. Had she heard me muttering?

I headed for the buffet, glancing at every woman's shoes. Zero, zilch, nada, no size eight and a halfs. Most of the women were already seated and eating. I couldn't very well crawl around the floor looking at people's shoes.

I said as much while I sat at the table.

"Why didn't you ask for my help?" Grandma waved a fried chicken leg in the air. "I have a pair of Thomas Madden of the right size, still in the box. We could do a giveaway. Any woman who signs up would obviously have the right size feet."

I grabbed her and planted a kiss in the center of her forehead. "You're a genius!"

"I tried looking while folks were lined up," Cheryl said, "but with my Sasquatch feet, it's kind of hard to know without outright asking."

"Does this entire table meddle in murder investigations?" Seth glanced up from his plate.

"Not me," Ted said. "I'm retired. If I want to enjoy my retirement, I have to stay as far away from Shelby as possible."

"Very funny." I scowled and focused on my chef salad. "Seth said I was an asset to the police."

"You got the first part of the word right."

It took me a moment to get his meaning. I threw my roll at him, bouncing it off his gray head.

"Please, no food fight in the dining hall." Alice joined us. "Stop causing trouble, Uncle Ted."

"Where have you been hiding, girl?" He asked.

"I have a lot of work to do." Dark circles were

under her eyes. She used her fork to push the food around on her plate. "Plus, I think I might have the flu. I can't keep much of anything down."

I studied her a bit more closely. The fine sheen of perspiration on her upper lip. The pasty skin. Weight loss. "Ted, do you still have that book on poison?"

10

"*N*o, it's in the evidence locker." Ted cocked his head. "Why?"

"I want to check something. I'll order a copy for myself." I pulled out my phone and placed the order, choosing one day delivery. Now, all I had to do was wait a day to investigate Alice's symptoms. "I think Alice should go to the hospital."

"Don't be ridiculous." Alice shook her head. "I don't have time for that."

"You could be poisoned."

"Nonsense. I don't fill my plate from the buffet. I fill it in the kitchen. I don't want to eat something that everyone else has had access to." She shoved her plate aside and stood. "I've work to do, as do you. Don't you have a social event tomorrow?"

Gee, thanks for the reminder, because I'm totally inept. I finished my lunch and headed for the storage room at one end of the community with Cheryl. We used it strictly for holiday decorations and party stuff. I needed everything I could find that would look good under a black light.

"Do you really think Alice is being poisoned?" Cheryl leaned against a stack of boxes.

I shrugged. "She might be simply worn down, but it should be checked out."

"If her uncle isn't concerned, then maybe we shouldn't be."

"Maybe. Look for white stuff." I shoved a box in her direction. If Alice didn't show up for the party tomorrow, or if she showed up looking worse than she did today, I'd be very concerned. "If someone was poisoning her, the question would be why? Other than being annoying, she stays out of people's business."

"What if she doesn't? What if she's sneaky and you just don't know?" Cheryl handed me two rolls of white crepe paper. "It's quite possible that she sticks her nose in the lives of the residents. You do."

"Good point." Arms loaded with decorations, we loaded everything into the golf cart and set off for the pool area. Heath had already told me he could put a black light in the pool. I hoped everything would look as ethereal as I envisioned.

It was just another pool party before the weather turned cool, but the difference in lighting would switch things up a bit, I hoped. If not, I could strike one idea off my list for the future.

"It looks like a white wedding," Gloria sang, twirling a streamer. "Wouldn't that be a hoot? Get someone hitched?"

"No, it would be a cruel joke and probably illegal."

She shrugged. "Why hasn't Heath popped the question?"

"I'm not ready. It hasn't been a year yet."

"That's the magic date?"

I stared at her while setting glow-in-the-dark lilies in the pool. "No, but less than that is too soon." While I loved Heath, truly I did, I wasn't ready for the commitment of an engagement. Not after my last fiasco. He didn't seem in a hurry either, which worked fine for both of us.

"I think I saw some floating candle holders in the shed." I tossed Cheryl the keys to the golf cart. "Can you go get them? They'll look nice floating around the lilies."

"Sure. Be right back." She hurried away, leaving me to finish putting out the water decorations.

As I leaned over the water, trying to right a flower that had filled and tilted, a hand shoved me in the back. I grappled for the side of the pool but went in anyway. Shoving my feet against the bottom, I shot to the top, only to find something holding me under.

I peered up through the shimmering water. Chlorine burned my eyes.

Leaning over the pool, one hand tangled in my hair, was a figure distorted by my splashing. Someone was trying to drown me.

I clawed at the hand holding me, then tried to pull the person in. When that didn't work, I went limp, sinking to the bottom. Play dead is what a person did with Grizzly bears, right?

My lungs burned. I couldn't stay down.

The figure disappeared and I shot to the surface. Weak from fear and near death, I dog-paddled to the pool steps and lay there like a grounded fish.

"Shelby?" Cheryl dropped the box she held and dragged me out of the water. "What happened? Did you fall in? Are you okay?"

"I was pushed. Someone held me under until they thought I was unconscious." I put a hand to my chest, thrilled beyond measure that my heart still beat, even if a little fast.

"Could you see who it was?"

I shook my head. "Not through the splashing."

"I'm calling Seth and Ted." She sat on the ground next to me and pressed numbers on her cell phone. She explained twice what had happened, then pulled me close into a one-armed hug. "I'm never leaving you alone again."

For once I was inclined to agree. Which, I knew, would only last until the trembling stopped.

Ted was the first to arrive. He squatted next to me. "What happened?"

"I heard Cheryl tell you on the phone. I'd rather not repeat it until everyone is here. It was traumatic enough."

"Fair enough." He grabbed a pool chair and sat down. "Haven't you had enough near-death experiences?"

I glared. "I was only doing my job! I wasn't investigating."

"Let me through," Seth said to no one in particular, since the three of us were sitting. "What happened?"

I sighed and recounted the story I'd told Cheryl, who had told both of them on the phone. "That's about it. I'm fine now and have work to do." I pushed to my feet.

"I think you need checked out," Cheryl said. "I can drive you to an Urgent Care or something."

"I didn't swallow any water." Since I was already wet, I slipped into the pool and righted the decorations I'd sent askew while thrashing for my life.

I glanced up to see tears in Cheryl's eyes. "You're so brave to go back in the water." Her voice cracked.

"It wasn't one of you who tried to drown me." Talk about drama.

~

I'd chosen to wear white linen pants and a white tank top to the party. I couldn't help but think how well I was going to stand out to the person who tried to kill me. Still, they'd find out soon enough that I was alive, kicking, and madder than a wet hen. God protect them when I found out who they are.

I stepped out of my room as Cheryl, wearing a white flowing dress, stepped out of hers. She eyed my outfit. "A whole lot of white going on."

"You said that earlier." I marched to the front door. "Ready for a lot more?"

"Are you running out of ideas for social events?"

"Yes."

"How about an auction? You could auction all the unmarried men for dates. These old ladies would give their entire savings for a date with Heath."

A thought, but not a pleasant one. "Keep the ideas coming." I locked the cottage behind us and headed for the pool. Always wanting to be the first one to arrive, there were plenty of last minute duties to perform, turning on the lights, making sure no decorations blew away, greeting the arrivals.

Grandma and Ted arrived next. From the way she hung on his arm, I guessed she had forgiven him for her brief time behind bars. Next came Heath, a lovely light in his eyes upon seeing me. Right behind him was my mother, then a horde of people, in white, and thankfully some fluorescent colors.

The kitchen staff wheeled in trays of food and set up a buffet on a table set aside for that purpose. To the enjoyment of the older crowd, I played old time band music. Right away a few cut away from the crowd and headed to a makeshift dance floor for some swing dancing.

"A great job again," Heath said, planting a warm kiss on my lips. "You should do this for a living."

I laughed and patted his cheek. "You look great in that white shirt." The black lights made the shirt almost transparent, giving me a clear view of a chiseled chest. My smile faded. Did that mean he could see through my clothes? I stepped into the shade of a tree.

"What's wrong?" He tilted his head.

"Nothing." I forced my smile to return. Maybe the black light wasn't such a good idea. I didn't want the party to turn into something inappropriate. I located Cheryl standing next to Seth who, thankfully, was out of uniform and wearing all black.

I pulled her aside. "Can you see through my clothes?"

"No, why?" Her eyes widened. "Tell me you can't see through mine."

I stepped back. "You're good." My pulse returned to normal. It was just the shirt Heath wore, and I didn't mind the view a bit.

Alice stumbled through the gate, looking like death on a plate. She held out her hand to me, then crumbled like a wounded butterfly.

Gasps and screams filled the air.

I rushed to her side, Ted right beside me. I felt for a pulse. Slow, her breathing erratic. "Call 911." I didn't need a book to tell me she'd been poisoned.

11

*T*ed glanced up from where he knelt beside his niece. "The book on poison is on my nightstand, Shelby. Find out who is behind this."

"Are you sure?" I looked over my shoulder at Officer Willis. "Won't I be interfering?" I planned on investigating anyway, but having Ted's go ahead would help a lot.

"I'll clear things with Willis." He stood and stepped back as paramedics arrived. "You have a gift, Shelby. Use it." He followed the gurney, with Alice lying still on top of it, to the waiting ambulance.

"You heard him," Grandma said. "Let's go get that book."

Unfortunately, there was a party going on. "That will have to wait until later. The residents are spooked enough. Let them have what fun they can." It would also give me an opportunity to see whether anyone seemed satisfied about Alice's misfortune.

Dean Roof and Madeline Cross, deep in a private conversation, kept sending covert glances in the direction Alice had been taken. Susan Hall and Lori Brown kept their heads down as they refilled food trays. Joyce stood off to one side keeping an eagle eye on her staff. All in all not very suspicious, but since they were the newcomers to Shady Acres, warranted the most of my attention. I still couldn't reconcile the notion that a long-time resident could be behind Lloyd's murder or Alice's poisoning.

Still, after watching multiple crime dramas on television with Grandma, I knew everyone was capable of violence under the right circumstances. I just needed to find out what the particular trigger was and for whom.

What did Alice and Lloyd have in common? I needed to get into the manager's office and take a look at the man's file. The police would have taken it, but I also knew Alice made a copy of everything.

"What's your plan?" Heath sighed. "I know you have one. I can see the wheels turning."

"Ted asked me to do this."

"Someone is always asking you to walk into danger and you never hesitate."

"I'm sorry." I put my hand on his arm. "I love seeing justice served and knowing I had a hand in bringing it to pass."

"So, what's the plan?" He asked again.

"First, we'll fetch the book from Ted's cabin, then I want a look at Lloyd's file. We need to find out what he and Alice have in common for them to both be targeted."

"Maybe there's nothing. Have you considered the fact that Alice might have stumbled across information that made her a target?"

"I have, and I need to know what that is."

The party was in full swing until almost midnight. By the time the area was cleaned, it was one a.m.

Fishing the master key from my pocket, I entered Ted's cabin, Heath, Grandma, and Cheryl right behind me. Behind them was Officer Willis, looking glum as usual.

"I cannot believe Ted authorized this," Seth grumbled. "This goes against every rule in the book."

"There are no rules where Shelby is concerned." Cheryl smiled and patted his cheek. "You'll get used to it."

I found the book on Ted's nightstand. With it tucked under my arm, I led the group to Alice's office. We would have attracted a lot less attention if I'd gone alone, or with only Heath to accompany me.

"I have no idea where Lloyd's file will be, so look everywhere." I sat in Alice's leather chair and opened the top drawer. Nothing but pens, pencils, and markers. A hoard of them in every color.

The bottom drawer was locked. "Does anyone know how to pick a desk drawer lock?"

"I do." Seth knelt next to me and jimmied the drawer open with a sharp tool hanging from his keychain.

While the drawer did hold files, it only held employee ones. I sighed and rolled my chair back, watching as the others riffled through a file cabinet and a bookcase. Wait. I ran my hand under the desk. Voila! A manilla folder with Lloyd's name was taped to the surface.

"I've got it. Let's head back to my place and see what we can discover."

"I can tell you what it says," Seth said. "Lloyd owned a general contracting business before selling it and retiring. He was quite well off."

"That's no reason to kill the man." There had to be something more.

"That's pretty much it, other than the fact that a client took him to small claims court a few years ago for an alleged back construction job on a porch."

"Who was the client?"

He shook his head. "The client died in a car accident shortly after the court date."

"Convenient. So the court thing is public knowledge, right?"

"Yeah, so?"

"Then there's no problem with me digging around in the transcripts." I grinned.

"I can tell you the details." He crossed his arm. "Dane built the new library. Have you noticed how the back awning leans to one side? The library sued him, won, and the man never got around to fixing the awning."

I needed to have a closer look at the library. "Why not?"

"He said the building was crooked. It isn't."

"Could he have been talking figuratively?"

His eyes widened. "I hadn't thought of that."

My grin widened. "I'll be taking some time off work tomorrow. Heath?"

"I wouldn't miss it." He slid his arm around my waist and led me from the office. "Neither, I'm sure, will Seth."

"Let him come. I'll show him how investigating is really done."

Heath laughed and walked me to my cottage as the others went their separate ways. Except for Cheryl and Seth. They spoke softly behind us, giggles and chuckles rising in the night air.

"Good night." Heath pulled me close for a kiss. "Morning will come quickly. See you at breakfast." He tweaked my nose and left, his long-legged stride carrying him down the walkway.

Once inside, I got ready for bed and scooted against my headboard, opening the book on poisons. Cheryl climbed into bed with me. Leaning on one elbow, she stared up at me.

"Do you really think we'll get lucky again?"

I narrowed my eyes. "What do you mean?"

"We caught a killer once…but almost died. What if we aren't as lucky this time?" She tapped the book. "That might tell you what poisoned Alice, but it won't tell you who did the deed."

"True, but it's a start. We have so little to go on. As for luck, we trust God. He promised to look after the foolish." Not that I thought what we were doing was wrong, far from it. I really believed I was making a difference in the world I lived in.

She sighed and rolled onto her back. "Turn off the light. I'm sleeping here tonight."

I did as I was told.

~

Immediately after breakfast, Heath, Seth, Cheryl,

and myself headed to the local library. Grandma had pouted a bit, but realized Ted needed her at his side while he waited for Alice to wake up. Mom, as usual, chose to stay out of the snooping, happier sitting safely behind her reception desk. I'd tried telling her we weren't snooping this time, but actually digging into a lead, but she said someone needed to hold down the fort with Alice in the hospital.

"What are you hoping to find?" Heath pulled the van he'd driven into the library parking lot.

"I'm up for anything that takes us a step closer to catching this killer." I shoved my door open and marched to the back of the library where what could have been a lovely red porch roof sagged on one side.

Why hadn't Lloyd repaired the roof? "Give me a boost?" I waved Heath over.

"I brought a ladder. It's safer." He put up the ladder and held it steady while I climbed.

On the second from the top rung, I craned my neck to study where the awning style roof attached to the building. It had pulled out by about three inches, leaving a hole large enough for me to get my fingers in.

Please, no bugs or spiders. I felt around until I came into contact with something smooth and cylinder in shape. Pinching it between two fingers, I pulled it out. "Lloyd had the roof sag on purpose." I held up my prize. "He'd hidden this inside."

"How do you know it was him?" Heath's eyes widened.

"Because he's the one that never fixed the roof. Unfortunately, I think the roof pulled away from the building more and more over the years, revealing the hole." I climbed down. "Let's open this in the van."

"Then it becomes evidence," Seth said.

"Of course, Officer Party Pooper." I yanked open the front passenger door and slid inside.

The others climbed into their seats and leaned close to me. With a deep breath, I pried off the lid and pulled out a sheet of wrinkled paper. It unrolled in my lap.

"A treasure map?" Dotted lines and an X completed what looked like a photocopy of an old pirate map.

"Except it says booze instead of treasure," Cheryl said.

"Prohibition?" Heath leaned closer, giving me a whiff of his woodsy cologne. I loved that smell. "Are there any prohibition houses around here?"

"Grandma would know. Let's head to the hospital. We can check on Alice at the same time."

"Did you look in that book last night?"

"You mean this morning?" I smiled, remembering what time I'd actually fallen asleep. "I glanced through it before breakfast. I think she was poisoned with foxglove. Another poison plant commonly found in gardens. We need to find out who at Shady Acres, besides me, knows their plants."

"How?" Seth sat back. "If the police haven't discovered the person, how do you expect to?"

"Oh, honey." Cheryl patted his hand. "Aren't you learning anything? Shelby goes where no woman has gone before and just finds things. Sit back and watch her work."

"I don't like any of this." He glowered and crossed his arms.

"Only because I'm a civilian." I glanced back.

"Well, yeah."

"Maybe I should get my private investigator's license."

"God spare us all."

Heath laughed and headed for the hospital. "Your sarcasm is only encouraging her."

I playfully punched his arm. "Hush. I'm serious. Maybe I should. If doing so gets me more police cooperation—"

"How much more do you want?" Seth groaned. "You're allowed way too much freedom as it is."

"Because the residents of Shady Acres trust me. Ted trusts me. People talk to me and I can go where you can't."

"It's against the law to keep a police officer from investigating a crime."

"Fine. I can go where you can't without flashing a badge." Touchy, touchy. "I tell y'all everything I find out. I don't see the problem."

"That's the problem!"

Gracious, the man had a temper. Cheryl wasn't helping either. All she did was sit in the back seat with him and grin like a loon. He wasn't that brilliant of a conversationalist.

I glanced at Heath and shrugged. He took my hand. "Don't worry about him. I've got your back."

I knew he did, too. He was always there when I needed him, helping me with patience and kindness, even if he didn't like what he was helping me with.

"Let's go see my grandmother about some booze."

12

Alice was awake and sitting up when we entered her hospital room. She frowned. "Who's working today?"

"It's good to see you, too," I grinned. "How are you feeling? Did the doctor tell you that you were poisoned with foxglove?"

"I'm fine, and no, he didn't. I want your garden plowed under."

"I don't grow foxglove in the food garden. It's a flower, and I intend to search the grounds for the plant."

"Good." She crossed her arms. "Uncle Teddy and your grandmother went to get coffee. Shall I call him to fetch extra?"

I glanced around my group. Everyone shook their head. "We'll wait. I need to speak with my grandmother." I pulled a chair closer to the bed. "Why would someone want to poison you?"

She turned away. "I have no idea."

"You're lying."

She sighed. "Fine. I found a map in Lloyd's cottage. I thought it might lead me to a lot of money. You know, like a treasure map."

"This map?" I showed her the photocopy.

"Yes, but I have the original. Or, at least I did. It disappeared from my office two days ago."

I groaned. Why couldn't we catch a break that lasted longer than five minutes? Now, we needed to find the so-called treasure before the thief who'd taken the map from Alice could.

"What a crowd!" Grandma stopped in the doorway and clapped her hands. "It's a party."

"Step aside, Ida." Ted, each hand holding a coffee cup, tried to squeeze past. "I see Shelby bursting at the seams to ask something."

I explained about the map, and its disappearance. "Grandma, do you know of any prohibition houses around here?"

She tapped a manicured finger against ruby-red lips. "That's not something folks would want to get out about their family history."

"Perhaps that is why the map was stolen and Lloyd killed. Someone wants the information kept secret." Hope swelled within me. "If we can find out who ran moonshine or other forms of illegal liquor during that time period, we might find the person responsible for the poisonings."

"It's the best lead we've got," Seth said, looking pleased. "Good job."

"How do we go about finding that out?" Alice

glanced from one face to the other. "I couldn't find out anything."

No offense, but she wasn't the bulldog I was. Once I got my teeth into a clue, I stayed on the trail—to the consternation of my family and friends, but they were getting used to me being in hot water.

"I got it!" Grandma snapped her fingers. "There's an old housing development that's getting ready to be renovated. The houses were all built during the Prohibition era. I've always wanted one of those houses. I bet that's where the loot is."

"I don't want to go during broad daylight. We'll attract too much attention," I said.

"No one is going without me." Heath gave me a stern look.

"Or me," Ted and Seth echoed.

Cheryl sighed. "It's quite the group for a secret treasure hunt."

I agreed. I needed to find a way for just me and Cheryl to sneak away. Rolling the map and then putting it in my purse, I stood. "I'm glad to see you're on the mend, Alice. It's time for us to get to work."

I motioned for the others to follow me. "I need to find the foxglove. We also need to come up with a plan for a suspect." If I went through all the cottages and studied the books on shelves and got into their computers, I might find someone with an interest in plants.

"What are you scheming?" Heath pulled me aside once we stepped out the hospital doors.

"Getting into the cottages. I'm trying to think of a place to begin."

"I'd start with the new residents and staff. We

know everyone else pretty well. If we don't find anything suspicious on the newbies, then we'll go with the others."

"Great idea. What reasoning can we use to get access?"

"Isn't that Mayor Tollson?" He peered over my shoulder. "Yep, and that isn't his wife he's kissing."

I spun around. Sure enough, our esteemed mayor, a man I've never met, was hot and heavy with a pretty young thing in a tight dress. "None of our business."

"Alright. Back to business. I can always use the excuse of preventive maintenance and you're there to take notes. Simple, but effective."

"Wonderful. I'll make up fliers and have Mom put in all the mailboxes alerting residents it will begin tomorrow."

He shook his head. "No, that will—"

"Alert the killer. Okay, we'll cold call everyone, so to speak."

We joined the others at the van and returned to Shady Acres. After locking the map in the safe, I joined Heath in the reception area where he filled Mom in on Alice's condition.

She listened with a rapt expression, nodding at the appropriate times. "I'm so glad she isn't another casualty. Sometimes, I wonder about accepting a job here. It's a very dangerous place to work."

"Not so bad." Heath grinned and turned to me. "Ready?"

I grabbed a clipboard from Mom's desk. "Ready."

"Where are you two going?" Mom gave me 'the look'.

"It's best you don't know." I raised my eyebrows.

"Ignorance is bliss in this situation."

"You're going to give me gray hair that not even Clairol can cover."

I gave her a quick hug and followed Heath to the elevator. Obviously, we were beginning with the apartments.

"I don't think we'll finish today," Heath said, pressing the button to take us to the second floor, "but we'll get a good start."

I never could understand why the rooms were number with 101, 103, etc., when on the second floor. The doors opened and we headed for Dean Roof's apartment.

Heath knocked, no answer, then knocked again. When still no answer, he pulled his keys from the ring on his belt.

"Can we go in without permission?"

"All the residents signed a waiver upon renting that says I can go in at any time for maintenance." He unlocked the door and pushed it open for me to enter first. "I'll lock the door so we have some warning if Dean returns."

I nodded and headed straight for a couple of books on the nightstand in the bedroom. Dean's apartment didn't look lived in except for the books, a corner of fabric sticking out of a partially closed dresser drawer, and a few toiletries I'd spotted on the bathroom sink.

The books revealed nothing more than that he liked to read the newest releases in Detective Mysteries. Not a single plant or pamphlet or book to show he was the slightest bit interested in poison foliage.

"Shelby!" Heath called front the front room.

I stepped to his side just as the door opened and

Dean entered. He stared for a moment, then asked, "What's going on?"

"Routine maintenance," Heath said. "Mark room 101 good."

I marked a check on the blank sheet in front of me. I really should have thought this through more thoroughly and printed off something official looking. With a smile, I clasped the clipboard to my chest and waltzed out of the apartment.

We weren't as lucky at Madeline Cross's apartment. She answered at Heath's lock.

"Everything is just fine. I've recently moved in," she said, barely opening the door. "I'm not expecting company."

"It's only a routine inspection," Heath said. "We don't mind a little mess."

She closed her eyes for a moment. "I suppose you'll only come back when I'm not here, right?"

Heath glanced at me. "Yes, ma'am."

"Very well." She opened the door and stepped back.

I could see why she didn't want anyone in. The times I'd seen Madeline at meals, she was impeccably groomed. The apartment, not so much. Clothes and papers were strewn over every available surface. The only thing that showed any sign of order was her bookcase. A large wooden monstrosity that took up one wall.

"You're a reader?" I quick stepped to the books, scanning quickly.

"Those are my treasures." Madeline joined me. "I read every genre. Even nonfiction."

"You have a few first additions, too." Envy filled

me. "What a wonderful collection." But nothing on plants. "Is this all you have?"

She chuckled. "Isn't it enough? I've run out of room it seems. The one thing this community lacks is a library. I'm thinking of asking Alice to donate an empty apartment as one."

She'd never go for losing the income. "That's a great idea. I, personally, enjoy books on plants."

"I don't have a green thumb, I'm afraid. Not like you. The gardens are quite lovely."

"Thank you." Nothing to be found here. I made a small motion to Heath, who nodded.

"Everything looks fine, Ms. Cross. Call me if you need any repairs done in the future."

"Thank you." She showed us the door.

Once in the hall, I leaned against the wall. "We're getting nowhere fast. These are the only two apartments rented at the moment."

"We'll have to check the cottages of the kitchen staff. That's all we have left."

I twisted my lips. "It's almost supper time. We'll have to postpone."

He took my hand. "I know you're planning on sneaking away to the houses your grandmother mentioned. I'm dogging your steps to keep you from going without me."

"Fine. I'm leaving as soon as it's dark. It's best to bother the residents and staff during daylight hours anyway. Should I pay a visit to the kitchen? See who served Alice lunch yesterday?"

"That's a great idea."

We headed downstairs where Heath, true to his word, followed me into the kitchen. All three of the staff turned to face us as we entered.

"We don't have time for special requests," Joyce said. "We're serving dinner."

"Only a question, please." I hugged the clipboard. Why did this woman intimidate me so? "Alice must have eaten something yesterday the rest of us didn't. Does anyone know what she might have had?"

"She asked for tea," Lori said. "I made her a pot and carried it to her office."

"From fresh leaves?"

"Ground." Lori cocked her head. "I made the tea myself."

"Did you leave at any time while it was brewing?"

She took her bottom lip between her teeth and nodded. "I had to use the restroom, then I took my break. I let the tea steep on my fifteen minute break."

I glanced at Heath. Someone had tampered with the tea while Lori was out of the kitchen. That was the most logical explanation.

"Am I in trouble?" Her chin quivered.

"Of course not." Joyce put her arm around the woman. "Shelby is only being a bully. My girls are not killers. Go question someone else."

Interesting how she hadn't put herself into that declaration, nor had Susan said anything. All we'd received from the other helper was glares.

"Were you working during Lucy's break, Susan?" I took a step backward.

"Yes." Susan stopped tossing salad. "I was inventorying the pantry at Joyce's request."

"You've taken up enough of our time." Joyce shooed us toward the door. "If you want to eat, get out. I will personally taste each dish if that makes you feel better."

It did, actually. Heath and I waited by the buffet as the trays were brought out. With the attitude of a teenager forced to eat broccoli, Joyce took a spoonful of each dish set out, then with a toss of her head, marched back to the kitchen.

Satisfied, I filled a plate with a pork chop, baked potato and salad. It wasn't until I sat down and started eating that I realized most poisons didn't take effect immediately, but over time.

I actually thought about taking my plate to my cottage and waiting to check on Joyce in an hour. My grumbling stomach urged me to take the chance on instant gratification. I cut into my pork chop.

Heath ate slowly, seeming to be in deep thought. After several minutes, he set down his fork. "I just realized something. Mayor Tollson has aspirations, political ones. So, why is he messing around with a woman who isn't his wife?"

"I doubt he expected to get caught."

"His family helped found Boonesville. I think I read that a relative of his was the very first mayor. Why risk all that?"

My fork paused on its way to my mouth. My gut told me we needed to do some history on Mayor Tollson.

13

Since Cheryl wouldn't leave Seth's side, and vice versa, Heath and I sneaked out alone to head to the houses being renovated. I wasn't naïve enough to believe that Seth wouldn't follow once he knew we were missing, so we needed to investigate as much as possible before getting caught.

I remembered the houses Grandma spoke of well. While they'd never had their full beauty during my growing up years, friends and I would sneak through broken windows and scare ourselves silly with ghost stories. One house actually had a dark stain on the wood floor that we were convinced was a blood stain.

I glanced up at that very house and shuddered. Lit by the moon, it towered over us menacingly. It reminded me of every tale of a haunted house I'd ever heard.

"This will be gorgeous when it's finished." Heath obviously saw the house with a different view than I did.

"It'll cost a fortune."

He laughed. "Come on scaredy-cat. Let's go treasure hunting." He grabbed my hand and dragged me toward the gaping mouth of a front door.

I felt as if I should be wearing garlic around my neck, a cross, and carrying a wooden stake. Instead, I sent up a quick prayer and stepped inside, defenseless except for a heavy flashlight. Which, by the way, would be useless against ghosts or vampires.

"Stop dawdling. We need to find what we're looking for before Seth gets here and takes it away." Heath stared up a curving staircase. "Do you think that's safe to walk on?" He tested the bottom step.

"Nothing in this house is safe." I turned right into a small room that might once have been a parlor. In any old movies about prohibition I'd seen, the houses contained hidden rooms and tunnels. I pulled on a sconce near the rock fireplace. It came off in my hand, covering my arm with dust.

I shoved the sconce in the hole I'd made and glanced around as if I were about to get caught doing something bad. Then, I moved to a bookcase. No books to pull on to trigger the case to move. Maybe I was living in a fantasy that only existed in the movies.

"Shelby."

I followed Heath's voice to a kitchen. It was the most recently renovated part of the house and that had to have been in the 40s. The appliances were gone, cupboard doors missing, but the size of the room was every chef's dream. The more I wandered through the house, the more I fell in love with it despite the dilapidation.

"Do you think this house is for sale?" I ran my hand over a wooden kitchen island. How many meals had been prepared there?

"It would be easy enough to find out. Why? You looking for a fixer-upper?"

I grinned. "I'm looking for something for you to fix up."

"It would be fun, wouldn't it?" He leaned against a panel on the wall and...disappeared. The wall closed back together.

"Heath!" I ran my hands over the spot where he'd been. What had he pressed on?

It then occurred to me that I was alone in a dark house full of spooks. "Heath!"

I aimed my flashlight toward the foyer. If I couldn't find the entrance to the secret place Heath went in the kitchen, although I knew it was there, I'd have to find another way to get to him. Alone. By myself.

My throat clogged. I could do this.

Behind the winding staircase was a small door. I pushed it open revealing a small hallway with rooms branching off each side. Servants' quarters. There wouldn't be a hidden passage.

I left the door open, showing I'd already checked there and went to the dining room. A door in the wall showed a small hall that led from the dining room to the kitchen. A short cut for servants.

In every room I entered, I ran my hands over the walls, hoping, praying, to feel a panel. I was batting zero. There was no other course of action to take other than to climb the stairs.

Now, I weighed a whopping one hundred ten pounds, and ten pounds of that was hair. The stairs would hold me, right? I stepped on the first step, then the second. So far so good. I made it halfway up before I heard a groan and crashed through.

I hit the bottom with a thud, twisting my ankle under me, and stared up at Heath. "I hate this house."

"Are you all right?"

"Not really." I groaned and sat up. "Where are we?"

He shrugged. "I thought at first it was the basement, but it appears to be the very thing we were looking for. A hidden room with shelves and shelves of mason jars full of alcohol." He held one under my nose.

I sniffed and recoiled. "That's some strong stuff. How do we get out of here?"

"I haven't figured that out yet. Sit tight."

Since I couldn't walk, I had no choice but to let him continue searching. While I waited, I tried moving my ankle. No can do. I wasn't a doctor, but I was fairly certain I'd broken it. My flashlight didn't work either, and Heath was moving further away.

Footsteps sounded overhead. Dust rained down on my head and face.

I pinched my nose to keep from sneezing.

Heath kneeled next to me. "Shhh. We don't know if it's friend or foe."

"Sounds so historic," I whispered, choking back a giggle. I tended to laugh when nervous, and there was no time like the present.

Heath clapped his hand over my mouth and shut

off his flashlight, casting us into total darkness.

My breathing quickened. I closed my eyes, then popped them open again as the footsteps drew nearer to the hole in the floor above us.

They stopped and a light shined down on us. "Heath? Shelby?" Seth's voice was the best thing I'd heard in at least five minutes.

"We're here," Heath said. "Shelby's got a broken ankle. We'll need help getting her out."

"Find anything?"

"Yep."

More footsteps, a groan, and Seth's light went out. I prayed it wasn't literally. Cheryl would be devastated.

Heath dragged me out of view of the hole in the floor and shielded me with his body. "We aren't alone," he whispered.

I'd kind of figured that out for myself.

A horn blared outside.

Running footsteps.

Two gunshots.

What in the world was happening up there?

Heath stood. "I've got to check on Seth."

I grabbed the front of his shirt. "Don't leave me."

"I'll be right here. I haven't found a way out yet." He planted a kiss on my forehead and stepped under the hole.

"Seth," he hissed.

A groan proved the other man was still alive.

"Are you alone?"

"Cheryl. In the car."

"We heard gunshots."

Seth scrambled away from the hole.

We were still left in the…wherever we were with

no way out. What if the shooter was still out there? What if Seth and Cheryl were killed?

"Stop thinking the worst," Heath said.

"How do you know what I'm doing? You can't even see me."

"You sigh really loud when you're worried."

I shrugged and kept my gaze locked on the hole above us. What seemed like an eternity later, Seth and Cheryl both shined lights on us and lowered a ladder.

"Here goes." Heath slung me over his shoulder, caveman style before I could object, and started climbing.

I felt ridiculous. "Put me down."

"You can't climb. Be still." He bonked my head on the floor as we climbed out.

Once we stood, or rather he did, on relatively solid floor again, he put me down, keeping an arm around my waist for support. "Let's get out of here." He helped me hobble to the car.

Outside, I got a good look at Seth. Blood stained his shirt and matted the side of his head.

"I'll be fine," he said. "But, we'll need a ride back to Shady Acres." He pointed to his car which leaned on two flat tires.

"I saw the shooter," Cheryl said. "When a black clad person dashed from the house, I slid down in the seat. I almost screamed when they shot out the tires. I did jerk though, and leaned on the horn. They ran off then. I literally save y'all's lives." She grinned.

"Which we are very thankful for." I hopped to the front passenger seat of Heath's truck." The other two would have to ride in the back or cram into the smaller seats behind us. They opted for the truck bed.

"Let's get you to the hospital," Heath said, starting the ignition. "We can discuss what we found once we get there."

"It'll all be gone by morning. Every single jar of moonshine."

He nodded. "But, we know it was there and can now find out who owns the house. We're getting closer to catching a killer." He tossed a wink in my direction. "Plus, I took pictures on my cell phone."

"You had your cell phone? Why didn't we call for help?"

"I was going to, but then Seth showed up."

"Oh." I sat back while we made the drive to the hospital. "I don't really hate the house. I still love it."

He patted my knee. "I know."

Heath and Cheryl fetched wheelchairs while Seth and I waited next to the truck. Half an hour later, we were wheeled to a curtained off room together where Seth received stitches and I was sent to x-ray.

Sure enough, my ankle was broken. An hour later, I had a cast and pain meds and sat back in Heath's truck while a delicious fuzzy feeling began sweeping over me.

Crutches were seriously going to crimp my style, as Grandma would say. "How am I going to solve this case with a cast on?"

"With my help." Heath smoothed my hair away from my face before closing the door. He jogged to the driver's side and climbed in. "You be the brains of the operation and I'll do the footwork."

"I like the footwork. I also like my bright pink cast, but it itches. Are their ants in there?"

"You're loopy. Let's get you home. I've called

your mother. Sue Ellen is staying with you tonight."

I smiled. "I love my mama."

He laughed. "I'd like to stick around and watch the meds take effect, but it's getting late. Two late nights in a row is too much for me."

Back at the cottage, Heath carried me inside where Mom fussed over me and fluffed pillows in my bed. I removed all but one under my head and one under my foot. I didn't need her there, not with Cheryl staying with me, but it was nice to be pampered.

Mom set a glass of ice water on the bed next to me, kissed my forehead, and left. As she was closing the door, she whispered, "I'm sleeping on the sofa. I'll hear if you make a tweet."

I smiled and closed my eyes. We'd taken another tiny step toward our goal that evening. I still felt as if the killer stood right in front of me, but I was too blind to see who it was. Cheryl couldn't tell if the shooter earlier had been man or woman. The only description she'd given was tall and skinny, because she was trying not be seen.

So, we had a tall, skinny person with a foot size of eight and a half. More than we had before. We also had a possible motive. I fell asleep dreaming of moonshine.

I woke the next morning realizing we still hadn't followed the treasure map. That meant the bottles of liquor might not be the real treasure.

14

"*H*ere." Mom rolled a scooter toward me when I entered the living room. "I rented this. It'll be easier than crutches."

"My foot is throbbing. I doubt I'll be doing much of anything today." Which would bore me to tears. If I took the pain meds, I'd be loopy and unable to concentrate. If I didn't take them, all I'd think about was the pain. "Is Alice back? I need to talk to her." I still had doubts she'd told us everything she knew about the case.

If all she had was a map, which someone stole, why would someone try to kill her?

"I'll get her." Mom narrowed her eyes. "You'd better be here when I get back."

I put up my hands. "Where am I going to go?"

"Where there's a will, there's a way." She gave me

another look on her way out the door.

Fifteen minutes later, she entered with a grumpy Alice and a grave faced Ted. Uh-oh. Something was going to hit the fan if Alice really did come clean about withholding information.

"I'll make coffee." Mom bustled to the kitchen.

"Sit, please." I motioned for them to sit in the two chairs facing the sofa I sat in.

Once they were settled, I speared Alice with a sharp stare. "First, are you doing okay?"

She nodded, not meeting my eyes."

"Great. As you can see, I'm not. I broke this following a lead." I refused to shift my gaze off her. The fact she squirmed was testament that she was hiding something. I decided to play it up, which wasn't a lie, really. "I'm in great pain. While I was lying in bed, unable to care for myself," Alice flinched, "it occurred to me that you're withholding information."

Ted cut her a sharp glance.

"Now, you may have had a map, and said map may have been stolen, but that doesn't seem like enough incentive for someone to poison you."

Mom handed us our coffees and pulled up a kitchen chair. "Speak up, girl. My baby was injured following a lead she got from you."

Alice jerked. "Ida told her where to go, not me."

"Are you keeping information from us?" Ted frowned.

"Fine! I have information showing that Mayor Tollson is a direct descendant of moonshiners. His family operated a speakeasy in the basement of the very house Shelby got hurt in." She crossed her arms. "Happy?"

"What type of information?" I sipped my coffee. Yummy with hot chocolate instead of cream and sugar. Just the way I liked it.

"A diary."

"Where is this diary?" Ted leaned forward, spots of color high on his cheeks.

"A safe deposit box at the bank." She hung her head.

"Let's go." Ted stood and took her by the arm.

"Wait." I set down my mug. "Why lie?"

"I wanted to solve this mystery myself." Tears shimmered in her eyes. "You're always getting the credit. I wanted some of the limelight."

"This foolish act almost got you killed." Ted pulled her toward the door. "You hang around Shelby too much."

She glanced over her shoulder and mouthed, "I made copies."

Good girl. I grinned, knowing she'd be back as soon as the diary was handed to Ted. I'd have something to read while I recuperated.

Alice returned an hour later, a stack of photocopied papers tucked under her blouse. "I had a hard time getting away from Uncle Ted. But, I faked tiredness." She set the papers on the coffee table.

"What are you two cooking up without me?" Cheryl entered the room with a serious case of bedhead. "I cannot believe I slept in. How glorious!"

"Your hair…not so much."

"Phooey. Who's going to see me?" She poured a cup of coffee and sat in the chair once occupied by Ted. "What's that?" She motioned with a bare toe at the papers.

"A diary showing our esteemed mayor is as crooked as a winding creek." I grinned.

"Crooked enough to kill?"

I shrugged. "At least crooked enough to hire someone to kill."

"Brush your hair," Mom told her, coming from the kitchen. "You don't sit in polite company looking like you crawled through a briar patch."

Cheryl rolled her eyes and headed to the bedroom. When she returned, her hair was in order and she wore shorts and a baggy tee shirt. "Happy?"

"Very." Mother smiled. "Let's divide these pages and start reading." She divided the stack into fours, giving us all about fifty pages to read.

Four pairs of feet were propped on the coffee table. The only sound was the rustling of papers and muffled thumps of mugs being set on the table.

I had the first group of pages, starting with the date of July 18, 1921, written by one Horace T. Tollson. The man seemed quite proud of the fact that he ran moonshine and operated several stills with his brother Homer L. Tollson.

"Oh, the house you fell in was built in January of 1922," Cheryl said. "This guy—"

"His name is Horace," I said.

"Horace is quite proud that his venture provided enough funds for him to marry a Lucy Halloway and build her the house."

"Shelby has the papers that prove the Tollson family made illegal liquor," Alice injected.

"Thank you, Miss Obvious." Cheryl shook her head. "He also hasn't told his new bride how he makes his money. What a silly, trusting woman."

"Well, she found out in my pages," Mom said, "and promptly left his butt behind. He's furious she moved back in with her mother and is one of those women carrying signs around town that says, 'Lips that touch liquor, shall never touch ours'. How quaint."

"We still don't have a solid motive to confront the mayor." I kept reading.

"She's pregnant in my pages," Alice grinned. "Of course, I've read the whole thing already, but don't want to spoil y'all's fun."

"Oh, no." Mom glanced up with tear-filled eyes. "Horace is threatening to take the baby away. A sweet little boy."

"Don't worry." Alice reached over and patted her hand. "Lucy leaves town."

"But..." I noticed the sad tone of her voice. "What happens in the last pages?"

Alice frowned. "Lucy dies under suspicious circumstances. Then, Horace takes little Junior and remarries. They never could pin Lucy's death on him, but he brags enough in the diary that I'm certain he killed her."

"How?" I was so engrossed in the story that I'd almost forgotten my aching foot until I shifted positions.

"She fell off a cliff while picking wildflowers."

"Likely story!" Cheryl slapped her pages against her leg. "He killed her because she made him look bad."

"Ladies, I think we have a motive for murder. If this story were to get out, Mayor Tollson would never get re-elected." I put my pages into a neat pile and added them to the others.

"What do we do with this information?" Cheryl asked. "Once someone knows we know, we can't eat anything not prepared by our own hands."

Been there, done that. I rested my head back against the sofa, ready for a pain med now that the distraction of reading a gripping true story was finished. "I'm not sure, but I'll come up with something."

Mom must have seen the pain on my face. She jumped up and brought me a glass of water and a pill.

"Thank you." I closed my eyes while the others speculated on how to confront the mayor. I hoped by listening I'd come up with a plan or one of them would.

"I say we come right out and ask him," Cheryl said. "Catch him off guard."

"No," Mom argued, "a kind word is better. Why not tell him we have the diary and see what he says?"

"What if he doesn't say anything?" Cheryl replied. "Unless we ask, he'll think we're a bunch of empty-headed women who don't know what his family did. We want him to come out and say his family were moonshiners."

"He'll never do that," I said, opening one eye. "Did I tell you Heath and I saw him kissing a woman who wasn't his wife?"

"Don't spread gossip, dear." Mom frowned.

"It isn't gossip when it's the truth."

"I didn't know he was having an affair," Alice said. "We could bring that up and slip in the information about his ancestors."

"You know what they say about a cornered animal." Mom stood. "I think you should give your ideas to Ted and let him deal with the mayor."

Of course Mom would say that. She'd wrap us all

up in bubble wrap and lock us in a closet if she could.

"I'm going to the dining hall to get lunch. I'll bring you back a plate, Shelby. You can catch a cat nap."

By the time she returned, I'd be fully asleep from the meds. Which was not a problem. I couldn't feel my foot when I was asleep.

When I woke, I was lying on the sofa, a pillow under my head, and light sheet over me. Heath sat in a chair, watching me.

He smiled. "Good afternoon, Sleeping Beauty."

"Hey." I tossed aside the blanket and sat up. "Where have you been all day?"

"Working. I carted away some loose clippings you'd left next to the walkway."

"Thank you. I was going to do that today until, well, you know." My stomach growled loud enough for him to hear.

"Here." He handed me a chicken salad sandwich. "I knew you'd wake eventually and be starving."

"You know me so well." I took a huge bite.

"I'd like to think so." He moved to sit next to me. "Cheryl filled me in on the diary reading this morning. Do you really think the mayor is behind the poisonings?"

"He's the only suspect I have."

"He's been a good mayor, Shelby."

"But if he's a murderer, he needs to be put away." I finished my sandwich. "Don't you agree?"

"I do. I just want us to be very sure before we approach him. Or better yet—"

"I know, tell Seth and let the authorities decide." My friends and family were starting to sound like a broken record. Maybe it was time to listen to them.

"How is Seth today?"

"A killer headache, but otherwise fine. Shall I call him to come over?"

I nodded.

He chuckled and kissed me. "Don't pout. It's the right thing to do, and you know it." He called Seth.

Five minutes later, a knock sounded at the door. "He must have been waiting around the corner," I said.

"No, just visiting Ted." Heath opened the door, allowing Seth and his uncle to enter.

"Give me the diary." Seth held out his hand.

"Hello, to you, too." I handed him the papers. "Would you like to hear what us women came up with?"

He glanced at Ted, who nodded. "I guess."

I explained our theory about Mayor Tollson wanting to keep it secret about his family's past. I then went on to tell him about Heath and I seeing him kiss a woman other than his wife. "Since he runs for office every year, I think this gives him a motive for murder."

Seth heaved a sigh. "It definitely puts him at the top of the suspect list. Giving us the diary and having us question him will take the target off you and the others. He'll think the police came to this conclusion on their own."

Relief washed over me. I really should have considered doing that before. I could investigate behind the scenes and let the police do the confronting. Yes, I think I much preferred that mode of action.

"I'll continue to fill you in as I uncover clues." I grinned.

Seth and Ted groaned.

15

*T*hree days later, Seth sat across from me at breakfast. "I spoke with the mayor. He said what happened in the past is the past and no reason for him to go to such lengths as poisoning someone. I believe him."

"We're right back where we started." I moved my scrambled eggs around on my plate.

"He was embarrassed, but didn't deny anything that was in the diary."

"Maybe he's a really good actor. I mean, politicians have to be, right?" I refused to let go of the thought that the mayor had something to do with what was going on. He had the most to lose, after all.

"Anything is possible." He stood. "I thought you'd want to know."

"Thanks." I shoved my plate aside and rested my

chin in my hand. Nothing else made sense. It had to be the mayor.

"Why the long face?" Cheryl, her second plate in her hand, sat down.

I told her what Seth had said. "I was sure we were on to something."

"What about Horace's wife? Or his son? Maybe there is a connection there."

"What motive? The only one who stands to be affected by relatives on the wrong side of the law is the mayor." I exhaled heavily.

"Don't get discouraged. You always figure out who did the deed."

"Yeah, when my life is in peril and I'm face-to-face with the killer." I still hadn't entered the tunnels again that ran under the community. After fighting for my life down there a few months ago, I didn't care if I ever went there again. It was hard enough going back in the maze.

"You're just discouraged because you can't get around like you want to." Cheryl grinned and bit into a piece of buttered toast.

"Maybe." We were back to snooping through residents' cottages on the slim chance of finding…something. Even that would be difficult on crutches.

"Let's do something completely different from finding a killer. Let's go to the movies."

I glanced up. "That would be a pleasant diversion."

"We'll see a chick flick comedy. Something to ease your pity party."

"I can't go until later. I have to get some work done. Maybe we could go to the last matinee?" Bushes needed trimming, the vegetable garden needed weeding, the list was endless.

"Sure." Cheryl grimaced. "I'll do the work while you supervise. You can't get down to do anything with a cast."

I smiled. "You're a great friend. I know how much you hate getting your hands dirty." A thunderstorm the night before had left the ground soggy. Pure torture for Cheryl.

Turns out she didn't need to get dirty. She smiled and batted her eyelashes and got some of the old men who lived at Shady Acres to do the work. I would always be in awe of the way she used her full-figured womanly skills to get men to do her bidding.

"I sure wish I had her power over men," Grandma said, stepping up next to the golf cart.

"You get plenty of male attention." I eyed her Lucille Ball hair and tiger striped leggings.

"Not when that buxom beauty is around." She eyed her chest. "Maybe I should get a boob job."

"At your age?" I rolled my eyes. "You're beautiful as you are. Ted thinks so, too." Good grief. She was in her mid-sixties. Way too hold to worry about how large her chest was.

Grandma preened and slid from the golf cart. "I think I'll go find the man who only has eyes for me." She tottered off on heels that would make a woman thirty years younger break an ankle.

When Cheryl finished reveling in her power, she drove the golf cart to the parking lot and helped me into her Toyota sedan. Thirty minutes later, popcorn and soda in hand, we sat and laughed through a matinee showing of a female comedy. It was just what I needed.

We stepped out of the theater to a setting sun. Since all I'd eaten since breakfast was buttery popcorn, it was no surprise my stomach growled loud enough to wake a sleeping bear.

"I hear you. How about some chili dogs?" Cheryl had me wait outside the theater while she rushed to fetch the car.

Watching a movie might not have moved me any closer to finding out who our killer was, but it did restore my spirits. I needed to take time off once in a while. Go on a date with Heath. We saw each other so much, we rarely went on what one would call a traditional date. We needed to make that a priority.

Cheryl pulled a few feet from me and exited the car to open the door. "Here you go."

"I'm perfectly capable of opening the door, but thanks." I slid into the front passenger seat.

Minutes later, I sat at an outdoor picnic table enjoying a chili dog and fries. No worries about poisoning at this meal. I ate with gusto, then stuffed, sat back and let out an unlady-like belch. "Excuse me."

Cheryl frowned. "Do you do that around Heath?"

"Of course not, but sometimes, you've got to let it out." I grinned.

"No wonder your mother is going gray." Cheryl grinned. "Let's go home." She picked up our garbage and walked behind me as I used crutches to get to the car. Once inside, she turned. "I only have two more weeks that I'm available to help you."

"I know, and we're getting nowhere fast." I clicked my seatbelt into place.

Cheryl set our drinks into the cup holders and started the engine. "Let's get up early in the morning and check the rooms of the kitchen staff. You and Heath never got to their rooms, did you?"

I shook my head. "You'll have to do most of the searching. I'll play lookout. It's a plan."

Cheryl chattered on about how much she liked Seth for what seemed like hours but was more like fifteen minutes. She stopped suddenly and glanced in her rearview mirror, slowing her speed as we approached a sharp turn in the road.

I passed the time halfway listening and sipping my soda until she looked a little too long in the mirror.

"What's wrong?" I glanced over my shoulder.

"I'm letting this jerk pass. He's been on our tail since the hot dog place."

"He isn't passing." Instead, the dark blue truck matched their speed. "Go faster."

"Not around this turn, I won't."

"As soon as we're around it. Maybe he'll back off or pass then."

He, I assumed it was a he because of the rusty old truck, didn't pass or speed up. Instead, just as we rounded the curve, he rammed our bumper.

Cheryl screamed and held tighter to the wheel. "Is he trying to run us off the road?"

"It looks that way. You'll have to speed up. We need to ditch him."

I tried to see whether it was a man or woman driving, but could only see an outline of someone wearing a baseball cap. I turned back around in my seat and held on to the strap near my head.

Tires squealed as Cheryl took the curve too fast. My heart beat in my throat, and I pressed a gas pedal I didn't have. Thank goodness the next stretch of road was straight. If not for the deep ditch on one side, we'd be relatively safe.

Still, the truck didn't back off. Another, harder ram and Cheryl and I headed straight for the ditch. Of course it had rained hard the night before. Of course the ditch was full of muddy water. Still, I closed my eyes and prayed the water would help cushion the crash.

We went over the edge and slid a good three or four feet. When the car came to a stop, and I determined that, other than wearing most of my soda, I was relatively unharmed, I glanced at the road.

The truck idled there.

"Are you all right, Cheryl?"

"Yes. What are they doing?" She reached for her door handle.

"No." I grabbed her arm. "Don't move. We want them to think we're unconscious. If they see we aren't, they might come down here and finish the job."

She paled. "Surely the driver didn't think a crash in the ditch would kill us."

"I really don't know what they're thinking." Maybe they'd hoped we would hit a tree or flip over and drown as brown water filled the car. Who knew the mind of a lunatic? "Just be still until they leave."

"What if they don't leave?"

"Look for a weapon." I opened the glove compartment. Lying there, waiting for me to grab it, was a screw driver. It would definitely work in a pinch.

"That's all I got. Don't you have a Tazor?"

"At the cottage. I haven't carried it for the last few months. I switched purses and it wouldn't fit."

"That's stupid!"

"No one was trying to kill me until now!" I handed

her the screwdriver. "Take it. I'll kick them with my plaster foot."

The truck engine revved above us.

We silenced and froze.

The truck sped away.

The adrenaline left me in such a rush that tears sprang to my eyes. We lived another day. I reached for the door handle.

"No," Cheryl said. "You'll let the muddy water in. Climb out the window."

I frowned. "Are you serious?"

"Perfectly." She lifted her chin and rolled down her window. "It's going to take a tow truck to get my car out of here. I don't want the inside to have to be overhauled. I'm a teacher. I don't make a lot of money."

I groaned and rolled down my window. After searching, and failing, to find my cell phone, I decided to climb outside. It took a bit of fancy maneuvering to get my cast onto the seat so I could perch on the windowsill. Once I did, I folded myself in half the best I could and dropped into the thigh high water.

"I'm not supposed to get my cast wet," I muttered, sinking a few inches into the mud. Once I stood stable, I reached through the window and spotted my cell phone sticking from under the seat. I grabbed it to call Heath.

"Someone ran you off the road?" His voice rose.

"We're fine, but we need a tow truck and a ride," I explained.

"Where are you?"

"I can't see the mile marker."

"Climb up where you can and call me back. Be

careful." Click.

He was beginning to get like Ted. I stared at the wall of the ditch, trying to find a way out. Nothing but gravel, grass, and mud. I'd slide down more than I'd climb up.

"Cheryl, you're going to have to give me a boost."

"Seriously?" She put her hands on her hips.

"Unless you have a better plan."

"I don't." She leaned against the ditch wall and let me climb up her like a monkey. "Ow! Watch the cast. You jabbed me in the side. Oh, my favorite blouse is going to be ruined."

"I'm sorry." I perched on her shoulders and peered up and down the road. No mile marker in sight. "I've got walk a bit. Will you be okay?"

She put her hands under my bottom and pushed. "I'll...be...fine. Just hurry."

I landed on my hands and knees. Getting up, I brushed the dirt from my palms, and started limping down the road. My podiatrist was going to have a heart attack when he found out how I'd caused the damage to my cast.

By the time I walked at least half a mile to find a mile marker, my foot screamed with pain. *Please, don't let me be causing irreparable damage.* The sound of a vehicle approaching had me straightening. When I saw it was a dark-colored truck, I dove into the bushes.

It wasn't the same truck. I sighed. If I hadn't have panicked, we'd have a ride right now.

I called Heath, gave him the mile marker number, and sat on a large rock to wait. Instead of my sweetie arriving, it was Cheryl's.

Seth parked on the edge of the road and rushed to

my side. "You look a mess."

"Thanks." Cheryl was going to die of embarrassment when Seth saw her.

He helped me into the car and headed to where I told him Cheryl would be waiting. When we arrived, he left me in the car and approached the lip of the ditch.

I could see his grin from there as he reached down to help my friend out. I could also see how red her face was. It almost made the near-death experience worth it to see her so discombobulated.

Almost, but not quite.

16

*H*eath and Mom were waiting at the Emergency Room entrance when Seth drove up. He rushed to help me from the car, wrapping me in a giant hug. "You scare me."

I sighed. "Sometimes, I scare myself."

Seth hadn't parked the car before Grandma and Ted arrived. Just like a family that was never apart, we trooped into the Emergency Room. The intake lady took one look at us and shook her head.

"You're becoming a regular here." She typed a few keys on her computer keyboard. "What's the problem this time?"

"I need a new cast." I pointed at the soggy, muddy mess on my foot.

It wasn't hard to see her struggling not to roll her

eyes. Her eyelashes fluttered like a strobe light. "Have a seat in the waiting room."

Heath helped me hop to a waiting chair, then sat next to me, keeping my hand in his. "Are you all right?"

"I'm fine." I laid my head back against the vinyl seat and closed my eyes.

"Never mind that." Seth pulled up a chair. "Tell me exactly what happened."

"We went to the movies. Got a chili dog. Got ran off the road by a dark blue truck. That's pretty much it." I didn't open my eyes.

"She isn't always the most helpful person," Ted said.

"I see that." Seth tapped me on the head with his notepad. "Wake up. I have questions."

"I'm not asleep." I opened one eye. "I can talk with my eyes closed."

"But it's harder to tell if you're lying."

The other eye snapped open. "Why would I lie?"

"I'm beginning to think you desire attention."

"Hey!" Heath stood.

"Settle down," Seth glared. "I'm entitled to my opinion."

"That is not true," Cheryl said. "We were driving down the road, minding our own business, when this…person in the truck tried to kill us."

"Did you get a look at him or her?"

"No, but they wore a baseball cap." She crossed her arms. "After running us into the ditch, they sat on the side of the road for a while. Shelby thought it smart for us to play dead so the person didn't come down to us. Then, we climbed out and Shelby went to find the mile marker. That's it. Nothing more to tell."

"What about the truck? Did you notice any scrapes or dents?"

"I've seen a dark blue truck in the parking lot of Shady Acres," Mom said. "Off to the side. By the dumpsters. I've seen it at least three times."

We all turned to stare at her.

"What?" Her eyes widened. "No one has asked me before."

True. Mom usually sat quietly on the sidelines and took care of me when I got hurt snooping.

"Are the residents required to give their license plate numbers?" Seth leaned forward.

"Yes." Mom smiled. "I haven't gone out and looked at the license plate number, though, but I can check to see if anyone owns a dark blue truck."

"That would be great." Seth grinned. "We might have a solid lead."

Which reminded me… "You're full of criticism in regards to what I find out, Seth. But, what have you done to find this killer?"

He looked taken back. "I cannot divulge details of an ongoing police investigation."

"Oh, phooey." Grandma shook her head. "We're all family here. You can tell us."

"No, I can't."

"Because you don't have any more information than we do." I gave a definitive nod.

When they called me to a back alcove for a doctor to put a new cast on my foot, I didn't let anyone come with me but Heath. I told the others to go home and we'd meet them at my cottage when we were done.

Heath was quiet for a while once we were escorted

back, but finally spoke. "I think I've seen that truck your mother mentioned. It's an old Chevy with a missing back bumper and a scrape down the passenger side. Does that sound like the one that ran you off the road?"

"I didn't look that closely, but if it is, it should have silver paint from Cheryl's car. Do you really think they'll park it at Shady Acres again? The driver obviously knew it was me inside." Which meant I'd know the exact truck when I saw it.

"I'm sure Seth will put out an APB. The truck will be hidden." Heath hung his folded hands between his knees.

"What's wrong?" I put a hand on his arm.

"The danger to you escalated this time. Usually, we have a better clue who the killer is before they try to kill you."

True. I took a deep breath and exhaled sharply. "I'll be careful."

"I know. You say that, but—"

"Trouble finds me." I rested back while the doctor entered, frowned at the mess I'd made of the cast, but without reprimanding me, got to work.

While he fixed what I'd manage to ruin, I gazed at the ceiling tiles and let my mind wander. If someone at Shady Acres had a dark blue truck, why hadn't I seen it? I drove the golf cart over the entire grounds practically every day. Of course, other than the time I climbed into the dumpster, I rarely went to that corner. That was where the kitchen staff frequented the most. I needed to talk to them again.

~

The next morning, Heath confirmed our suspicions

that the truck hadn't been returned to the parking lot as he helped me to the dining room for breakfast. "Other than an oil stain, there's no proof a vehicle was ever parked there."

"Maybe Mom will find something in the resident files." I sat in the chair he pulled out for me.

"We can hope. Ham and cheese omelet?"

"With bacon and mushrooms." I grinned, not caring that bacon and ham were a bit redundant. Joyce would roll her eyes when Heath gave her the order, but she'd make it for me. She always did. "Oh, and ask her to come speak with me when she's finished, please." Other than clump my way to the kitchen, I'd try to get the staff to come to me.

Joyce didn't join me until almost an hour after breakfast was served. When she did sit down, she wore a scowl. "What now? I'm busy. Susan took a vacation and the temporary help hasn't arrived."

"When did her vacation start?"

"This morning. Why?"

"Do you know anyone who drives a truck?"

She tilted her head. "A lot of people drive trucks, Shelby. You'll have to be more specific."

"Do you know anyone who drives a dark blue, seen better days, truck?"

"I've seen one around, but I have no idea who owns it. I have an old Nissan. Susan drives a Mini Cooper. Lori drives a Sentra." She raised her eyebrows as if to ask whether I had anymore stupid questions.

"Did Susan leave town for her vacation?"

"She isn't staying here, if that's what you mean." She planted her hands flat on the table and stood. "I have work to do." She marched to the kitchen, leaving me alone in the large dining room.

I huffed and grabbed my clutches. Mom was my last hope at finding that truck. As I slowly made my way to the reception entrance, it occurred to me that I was completely alone. No one in the dining room, no one on the walkway outside. Just me, hobbling along in a slow clumsy way. I was easy pickings if the killer was close by. I really needed to insist that Cheryl spend less time with Seth and more time with me.

The man had a job after all. She didn't need to sit around waiting for him to call on one of his breaks. I needed her as my bodyguard.

Feeling as if the target on my back was as large as the building, I opened the door to the reception area and shuffled inside. Mom was bent over, thumbing through files in a bottom drawer. As I clumped toward her, she turned and let out a small squeak.

"You scared me." She put a hand to her throat.

"What are you afraid of?" I sat down, leaning my crutches against the wall.

"That I'd get caught helping you and someone would try to kill me." She avoided my gaze. "I'm not as strong as you, Shelby. I'd never escape."

"Don't be silly. All you're doing is looking for the license plate number of a resident. Did you find anything?"

"The only trucks registered to residents here belong to Bob Satchett and Marvin Hall. Both dark green trucks." Her cheeks brightened.

I narrowed my eyes. "Bob's a hothead, and Marvin's an ex-con, but I don't think they'd try to kill me."

"Neither do I." She sat behind her desk and smiled,

eyes twinkling.

Something was up. "What's wrong with you?"

"Nothing."

Her tone said the opposite. "Oh, my gosh! You have a crush on one of them."

"I'm too old for crushes, dear."

"You have been suspiciously absent at some meals. Which one of them are you seeing?" Mom, dating. I wasn't sure how I felt about the idea.

She ducked her head. "Bob."

"Bob! Of all the people in Shady Acres, why date one with a short fuse?"

"He's quite sweet."

I thought I was going to be sick. "I think it's time for another poker night."

"Don't give him the third degree." Her eyes went from twinkling to flashing in a split second. "I like him, Shelby. I don't want you running him off."

"I'm not a teenager who wants her mother all to herself." Well, I did, but I wouldn't ruin what happiness she could find after Dad's death. If anyone deserved it, Mom did. But, Bob Satchett?

"If you really want to find out who owns that truck, you should ask the vampire."

Of course. Leroy Manning, a resident with a skin disorder that prevented him from going outside during the day, knew everything that went on. I gave myself a mental palm slap against the head. "Thanks, Mom. I'll go talk to him right now."

I made my way to Leroy's. He must have seen me coming because the door opened as I reached it.

"Shelby!" He grinned and ushered me inside. "Fill me in on the latest. It's been too long since I've seen you."

"I'm sorry about that."

"Trying to find out who is poisoning whom?"

"Yes." I sat at his small dinette. "You wouldn't be able to help me, would you?"

"What do you need to know?" He poured me a glass of tea and stirred in two teaspoons of sugar, knowing how I liked my drink.

"Do you know what foxglove looks like?"

"Sure do." He walked to a bookcase in the corner of the room and pulled a book off the shelf. "I like to study plants."

"Have you seen any growing around here?"

"There's a few flowering plants in the maze." His eyes widened. "Did someone ingest some?"

I nodded. "Alice. Lloyd Dane was killed with Fool's Parsley. I've already removed what I found of that. Then, last night, someone in a dark blue truck ran me and Cheryl off the road."

"The blue truck that's usually parked by the dumpster?"

"Yes. Do you know who it belongs to?"

"Nope, but I don't think it's anyone who lives here. It's not there all the time."

"If you see it again, will you write down the license plate number?"

"I'll do that and let the air of the tires." He grinned. "If they can't drive away, you'll catch them."

If only it were that easy.

17

*T*hree days had passed and no blue truck. Susan was back at work in the kitchen driving a small green Honda that had seen better days. I was back to square one and feeling quite sorry for myself.

"What's up, buttercup." Cheryl plopped on the sofa next to me. "Someone run over your dog?"

"Hush. I don't have a dog." Maybe I should get one. A big one. A companion to be at my side at all times and help keep me out of trouble.

"What's wrong?" Her smile faded.

"Nothing, really. I'm bummed about my foot, I don't have a single suspect in the poisonings, and Grandma's sixty-fifth birthday is coming up and I don't have anything planned."

She patted my leg. "The foot will heal. You'll

catch the bad guy. You always do. As for Grandma…plan a big formal shindig for this weekend's social event. Everyone will attend and she'll be pleased as punch to dress up."

"I don't have anything to wear."

"Wow, you really are having a pity party. Well, I'm not interested in attending that type of party. Put on your shoes, uh, shoe, and let's go shopping. I know the perfect little boutique."

I sighed, a bit dramatically, even for me, and limped to the bedroom to put on something other than baggy shorts and an over-sized tee shirt. By the time I was ready, my mood had improved a fraction, since shopping was always nice. I texted Heath and Alice to tell them I would be gone for an hour or two, and rejoined Cheryl in the living room.

"I need to make a stop at the nursery to order mulch. I could do it over the phone, but since we're going to be in town anyway, we can make a stop." I grabbed my purse and a crutch.

The closer we got to town, the more my mood improved. I really, really needed to get away from Shady Acres more. "Let's stop at the party store, too. I want the party to be formal, but traditional, complete with multi-colored balloons and streamers."

"That's cool," Cheryl said, pulling into the parking lot of the party store. "Kind of a mix between a kid party and an adult party. What about traditional games like Pin the Tail on the Donkey?"

"Great idea." I exited her car and clunked my way into the store where I filled a basket with balloons, streamers, and the game. What else could we do for fun? "Karaoke!" I bought a karaoke machine, hoping

Alice wouldn't have a coronary. She had given me a budget for monthly parties and I was careful not to go over. I added some old type favorite songs and paid for the purchases.

Our next stop was the nursery where I placed an order for several bags of mulch. We stepped back onto the parking lot as a dark blue truck rattled by.

Cheryl and I glanced at each other and rushed to the car. "Follow that truck." I clicked my seatbelt into place as Cheryl squealed tires in pursuit.

Adrenaline burned through me as my best friend drove with a skill to set many a race car driver to shame. "I hope that's the right truck."

"What?" She cut me a quick glance. "It might not be? I could get a ticket for nothing? There's been a police car flashing its lights for the last two miles."

"You'd better pull over. I think it's Seth."

"I know! That's why I'm not stopping."

"I really think you should pull over."

"Fine." She whipped the wheel to the right, spraying gravel. She brought us to a safe stop and rolled down her window.

Seth walked up and glared for several seconds, not saying a word. I could see mine and Cheryl's reflections in his mirrored sunglasses. He took a deep breath and shook his head. "Would you mind telling me why you were going eighty-five miles an hour?"

I leaned across Cheryl. "We were chasing a dark blue truck like the one that ran us off the road."

"I'll meet you back at Shady Acres later." He dashed back to his car and sped down the highway.

"That was easy." I laughed. "Now, let's go buy me a formal gown."

"Seeing Seth behind us scared me more than the time we were locked in that burning shed." Cheryl pulled back onto the pavement and continued toward town.

On Main Street, nestled between the pharmacy and an antique store, was a boutique called Fashion Treasures. A place that sold new and used one of kind gowns. I'd never had a reason to step inside before and looked forward to finding a dress only I would own.

In the window was displayed two mannequins. One in a simple black dress and one in a flowing red one. "I want the red one."

Cheryl gave me a look that clearly said I was out of my mind. "You're too petite to carry off something flowy. Me, on the other hand…" She marched straight to the clerk and asked to try on the dress.

I narrowed my eyes. Fine. I flipped idly through a rack of dresses. "This one." I held up a long royal blue gown that shimmered with the light.

"Oooh, perfect. Go try it on." Cheryl gave me a shove toward the dressing room, almost knocking me off my crutch.

I gave her a dirty look and made my way to a curtained off dressing room. After shedding my jeans and tee shirt, I slipped the gown over my head. It could have been made for me. The bodice fit like a glove, skimming the hips. The hem fluttered around my ankles. I felt like a princess. One glance at the price tag of two hundred fifty dollars had me choking.

"Let me see," Cheryl ordered.

I stepped out. She looked regal in the red gown. "That's gorgeous."

"Not as gorgeous as the petite royalty standing in

front of me. Wow."

I preened and swayed from side to side. "It's expensive."

"It'll be worth it for the look in Heath's eyes."

~

I had texted Heath on the way home and had him meet us to help unload the packages. It wasn't something I would have normally done, but without the use of two good feet, I wasn't much help with anything physical.

He eyed all the boxes of party supplies, and huffed through his nose. "I might as well take these straight to the dining room. That's where you'll hold the party, right?"

"Thank you." I blew him a kiss and headed into my cottage to make up the fliers for Saturday night. Since today was Thursday, I was cutting it close. Still, I was confident the residents would show up in droves for Grandma.

While Heath and Cheryl unloaded the trunk of the car, I made up a quick flier and made my way to the reception desk so Mom could make copies and put in mailboxes.

"She'll love this, Shelby. What a wonderful idea." Mom smiled and placed the flier on the copier. "I'm going to have Bob wear a tux."

"What are you going to wear?" I leaned against her desk, resolved to the fact that she was seeing the resident hothead and determined to be an adult about it all.

"I have a gown I wore to a charity event two years ago. It makes me feel pretty."

I remembered the dress. Tea length, flowing, and

the color of a rich red wine. It suited Mom perfectly.

"I'll come to your place early enough to tame your hair."

"I'll be glad for the help."

When I returned to my cottage, Seth had joined Cheryl and Heath. He motioned for me to have a seat. "The truck was the one that ran you off the road. The driver said it had been stolen, but since he found it by lunch time, he thought maybe he'd forgotten where he parked it and never filed a report."

"You believe him?" I propped my foot on the coffee table. "Sounds bogus to me."

"It's an eighty year old man who drinks too much and has no idea who you are. So, yes, I believe him." He turned to Cheryl and handed her a piece of paper. "Here's your speeding ticket." He stood and squared his shoulders.

Cheryl's eyes widened and her mouth dropped. She snapped it closed. "Are you serious? We helped you solve a bit of this case by eliminating…the old man. Yeah."

"You were going fifteen miles over the speed limit, Cheryl. You can take an online class and not have any points on your insurance. I'll see you at supper." He turned and left.

Cheryl pointed at me. "You're taking the class. This is your fault. You'd better pass it, too." She stood and stomped to her room.

I was pretty sure it was illegal to take the driving course for someone else, but I would at least sit there beside her for however long it took. "Back at the beginning again."

"Maybe this is one you should leave to the police."

Heath moved to sit next to me. "You're coming up against a wall and putting yourself in danger."

"I hate not finishing something." I leaned my head on his shoulder.

"I know, but I like having you around." He kissed the top of my head. "I'm keeping my eyes and ears open for you, but I'm coming up empty, too."

I couldn't stop thinking that I was missing a clue right in front of my face. The killer was at Shady Acres. I knew it in my gut. The problem was that I had no idea how to draw the person out into the open.

"Let's go eat." He stood and held out a hand to help me up. "Maybe if you take a few days off from thinking about this, what you're missing will come to you."

"I hope so. I'm feeling like a failure."

He chuckled and pulled me close for a hug. "You solved two mysteries and it went straight to your head. You aren't a detective or a police officer. You're a dark-haired Nancy Drew. Be patient. No one else has died."

I rested my cheek on his chest and counted his heartbeats, one, two, three. "You're a very patient man, Heath McLeroy. I'm a lucky woman."

"I agree." His chest rumbled.

Banging came from the bedroom. Cheryl shouted something, then another bang.

I laughed. "She must be thinking of her ticket."

"Let's leave before she chucks something at our head." He scooped me into his arms, then slipped his hand through my crutch. "I could get used to carrying you around."

"I might let you do it for the rest of my life." My

face heated as I thought of how my words could be interpreted. When Heath didn't respond, I relaxed and let him carry me to supper.

I couldn't help but let my mind wander to the mystery as I ate and my family and friends chatted about their day. Cheryl didn't stay mad long, instead talked about the dress she'd purchased that day and how much fun the party would be, if Seth could stay nice for one night.

"Nice?" He frowned. "I'm always nice. I can't play favorites with my job, Cheryl."

"Oh, pooh. Yes, you can. I bet Ted did with Ida all the time."

"Did you forget Teddy had a part in my stint in jail?" Grandma waved her fork. "It's not a laughing matter. These policemen are serious. Let them have their way. Making up is always fun, if you know what I mean." She wiggled her eyebrows.

I gagged at the mental picture.

18

I looked good! I smiled at my reflection in the mirror. Yesterday, the doctor had put me in a walking boot. No more crutches. The boot interfered with me wearing cute shoes, but it was better than clunking around on crutches in an evening gown.

Mom had fought with my hair, and won, styling it in a fancy up-do. With the amount of hair spray she'd used, my hair wasn't going anywhere. The hair, combined with the gown, made me actually feel pretty. I grinned and headed to the living room to meet up with Cheryl.

In gold heels, she towered over me more than usual. She eyed the one flat white sandal on my foot. "Pity." She shrugged and twirled. "How do I look?"

"Like a queen." I linked my arm with hers. "Where

are our men?"

"Late. Seth texted me and said he had to check out a domestic disturbance, they're short-staffed, then he'll be here and meet us at the party. I'm not sure where Heath was."

A knock on the door answered the question as to where Heath is. I opened it, and lost my breath. The man standing in front of me, in a tux, deserved to grace the cover of a magazine. The appreciative look in his eyes said he thought the same about the way I looked.

"Sorry I'm late." He gave me a quick kiss. "I couldn't get my tie straight."

"I would have fixed it for you."

"You're a knock out, Shelby. I don't think I tell you that enough." He put his hands on my waist. "Turn around, Cheryl, I'm going to mess up my date's hair with a heated kiss."

"Don't you dare." I laughed and put my hands on his chest. "A kiss for sure, but it took Mom a long time to get my hair to behave."

Cheryl grinned. "I'll see you two at the party." She sailed out of the cottage.

"Let's skip the party," Heath said, his eyes darkening. "I don't want any men looking at you."

"Grandma would kill me." I smiled. "Are you going to kiss me or not?"

"Oh, I'm going to kiss you." He lowered his head and pulled me close. His kiss, tender and first, then demanding, left me breathless and my knees weak. I never wanted it to end.

He pulled away and leaned his forehead against mine. "You send my heart into overdrive, Shelby Hart."

"No more than you do mine. We'd better leave

before we get into trouble. I need to beat Grandma there."

He groaned, gave me another quick kiss, and tucked a strand of hair that had fallen loose behind my ear. "Then, off we go." He crooked his arm.

I slipped mine through his and let him lead me to the party.

Balloons drifted across the expanse of the floor. Streamers in every color of the rainbow hung from the ceiling tiles. A disco light sent shards of iridescent light across everything, and the tables were full of laughing people in formal wear. A great contrast of childhood and the golden years.

"This is great," Heath said, leading me to our table. "You've outdone yourself."

"I had a lot of help, thanks to Cheryl." I grinned at my friend.

"It's ridiculous." Joyce glowered, refilling the water pitcher on our table. "It's a nightmare carrying trays of food with all the balloons underfoot."

"It's only for one night." I refused to let her mood ruin mine.

"It's a pain in my behind." She stormed away.

I shrugged and kept an eye on the door for Mom's signal that Grandma was approaching. When she waved, everyone stood and broke out into applause when Grandma entered, looking radiant in a long black gown. Tears filled my eyes. How I loved the old woman and thanked God for every day He let me spend time with her.

Ted escorted her to our table, tears streaming down Grandma's face, despite her smile. "Oh, Shelby." Her words broke on a sob. "Thank you."

"You deserve it, Grandma. I love you." I wrapped my arms around her and squeezed.

In honor of the celebration, Alice had approved additional kitchen staff. No buffet tonight. All the guests were to be served chicken parmesan, Grandma's favorite. Two men, both plain enough to blend into the background in their black and white uniforms, joined Susan and Lori in passing out dinners.

One of them, a man who looked to be nearing forty, exchanged a long look with Susan. Did I detect a hint of romance in the air? The two skirted around each other like strangers, tossing glances back and forth. When the man's gaze landed on mine with a deep intensity, I drew back.

Why the hateful look? I didn't think I'd met him before. I turned away first and concentrated on my caesar's salad. A few seconds later, I peered from under my lashes, relieved that the man had moved to the other side of the room.

"What's wrong?" Heath whispered in my ear. "I worry when your smile fades."

"It's nothing." I forced a smile, trying to ignore the feeling that I was being stared at. "The food is good."

"Let's hope no one gets poisoned tonight." He tapped my nose.

What a way to ruin an appetite. Although, it didn't seem to affect his.

"Sorry, I'm late." Seth rushed to the table and sat beside Cheryl. "I had to wrestle a man while wearing this monkey suit. Not easy without getting mussed."

Cheryl wiped at a spot on his shoulder. "At least you made it."

He grinned and waved the waiter over. The man

who looked at me as if he hated me, set a plate in front of Seth, glared at me, then left.

"Okay." I tossed my napkin down. "That man keeps glaring at me, and I have no idea why."

"Do you want me to talk to him?" Heath started to stand.

"No, we'll just keep an eye on him. He's been hanging with Susan when he isn't shooting daggers my way."

"I feel like I need to talk to him," Heath said, staring at the waiter.

"Don't cause trouble at my party." Grandma pointed at him. "No mystery solving, fights, or drama tonight."

"Yes, ma'am." Heath winked. "We can hold off until tomorrow."

In the corner, a small band tuned their instruments. When finished, the lead singer sung a slow ballad, providing romance to the meal.

"Dancing." Grandma clapped her hands. "I love dancing."

Ted groaned. "She'll make me dance every song, too."

"Not every song. Heath and Seth can take a turn." Grandma lifted her goblet of wine. "A toast, to my wonderful granddaughter who set this up for me."

"Hear, hear," the others said, raising their glasses.

My face heated. "Go on, no, really, go on." I grinned.

"That's enough," Grandma said. "I'm the guest of honor tonight. Shelby can have next month."

I laughed and sipped my ice water. Nothing made me happier than to see the ones I love enjoying themselves.

When we'd finished eating, the band started more lively music. Heath stood and took my hand. "Let's dance."

"With a boot on?"

"I'll help you." He led me to the area cleared for dancing and lifted me off my feet, swinging to the beat.

I tossed my head back and laughed.

Heath kissed the hollow of my throat and I forgot why I was laughing.

Soon, the floor filled with dancing couples. Mom sailed by in the arms of Bob. I still couldn't wrap my mind around them as a couple. Grandma smiled into Teddy's face, and Cheryl, an inch or two taller than Seth in her heels, bounced past, a bit out of time to the music.

Heath twirled me past the evil-eyed waiter. I met the man's gaze over Heath's shoulder. I refused to let the man intimidate me, and I would confront him at the first opportunity. Enough was enough. If I'd wronged him in some way, I wanted to make amends. If not, then I deserved an explanation for the glares.

"I'm right here," Heath said, using his finger to turn my face toward his. "Where are you?"

"Still wondering why that waiter hates me."

He set me on my feet, then took my hand. "Let's go find out. You won't enjoy yourself until you do."

The waiter ducked into the men's room when he saw us coming. I shrugged. We'd catch him later.

"It's time for some games."

Grandma totally cheated at Pin the Tail on the Donkey. She tilted her head back and pinned the tail in the exact spot. The next game, one where you have to wear a tag on your back of a famous person, real or fictional, was a bit harder

"Do I wear a crown?" she asked. "I should wear a crown. It's my birthday."

"No crown," I said for the third time.

"What color is my hair?"

"Yes or no answers, Grandma."

She sighed. "Do I have blond hair?"

"No."

"Do I wear a glass slipper?"

"That would make you Cinderella, if you were blond, who wore a crown."

"Not all the time! She was a scullery maid."

My head started throbbing between my eyes. "Why don't you ask some other people questions?"

"I'm perfectly comfortable sitting here drinking my wine and talking to you. Why aren't you wearing a tag?"

"Because I made the tags." I almost wished I was a lover of alcohol. "Where's Ted?"

"Trying to figure out who he is." She tapped a scarlet nail against her lips. "Black hair?"

"Yes."

"Blue eyes?"

"No."

And on and on we went for twenty minutes until the proverbial lightbulb went on over her head. "I'm Elizabeth Taylor! Of course. My favorite."

Finally. "Ding ding. You got it right. Are you ready for cake?"

"I'm ready for presents. Where do I sit?"

"The table near the door. We'll sing, you'll blow out the candles, then we'll do presents." I made my way to the door and cleared the table of the sign in book and feathered pen.

Once I had Grandma ensconced on her throne, a folding chair decorated with balloons and streamers, I motioned for Joyce to bring the cake. Lori helped her carry the three-tiered vanilla cake with a sugar crown on top.

Everyone gathered around and sang, "Happy Birthday" as the lights dimmed.

Grandma closed her eyes and blew out the sixty five candles lining the top of the cake. She did it in three tries to thunderous applause.

Guests approached and laid gifts in front of her as if she truly were the queen of Shady Acres. She received everything from books, to costume jewelry, to gift cards for restaurants. With each gift, her smile grew.

When she finished, everyone stomped on balloons, filling the room with loud popping. We covered our ears, laughed, and stomped.

Until the death glare waiter entered the fray and pointed a gun at my head.

Then silence reigned.

19

I stared down the barrel of a 9-millimeter Glock. Very similar to my own gun, as a matter of fact. Out of the corner of my eye, I saw Seth and Heath take steps toward me. I motioned them back with my hand as Death Glare moved the gun in their direction.

Wanting his attention back on me, I asked, "Do I know you?"

It worked. The gun swung back toward me. "Yeah. I'm the one that ran you and your big friend off the road."

"Hey!" Cheryl yelled from behind me.

"You're ruining my birthday," Grandma said. "Let's be reasonable. Have a piece of cake and talk things over."

Death Glare pointed the gun closer to my head.

"Why did you try to run us off?" I don't think I even blinked as I stared at the gun. "What have I done to you?"

"You're nosey."

True, but that didn't mean I should be shot.

He motioned the gun toward the door. "Walk backward real slow. If anybody tries to stop us, I'll shoot them, then you. Got it?"

I nodded and started moving toward the door. My brain whirled, trying to come up with a way out of the situation that wouldn't result in anyone getting shot.

I met Heath's gaze, his face pale. A muscle ticked in his jaw. I implored him with my eyes not to move.

Seth started to reach inside his shirt.

Death Glare raised the gun and shot out the disco light, plunging the room into darkness. He grabbed my arm and dragged me out of the building.

Chaos erupted inside. Shouts, gasps, and thundering feet echoed.

Heath and Seth barged outside, stopping in front of the door. Both steely-eyed gazes locked on me and my captor.

As Death Glare shoved me inside a van, my gaze locked with Heath's. *Please, Lord, don't let this be the last time I see him.*

Heath shouted, "No," then ran toward us.

Death Glare slammed the door, leaped into the driver's seat, and roared from the parking lot, with me bouncing around in the back of the van like a can of peaches. Through the back window, I could see Heath sprinting after us while Seth pulled out his cell phone.

Help would be coming. I just had to stay alive long enough. Now, to formulate a plan. An evening gown didn't leave a lot of room for movement, especially in a van barreling down the highway.

I got to my hands and knees and scrambled around looking for a weapon. My hand wrapped around a length of chain. Could I? Could I really wrap this around his neck and pull? It was worth a try. If I was going to die, then I'd die fighting.

Kicking off my heels, I slid up the inside panel of the van and got my balance. The chain made a small clink. I froze. When Death Glare didn't turn, I took a small step closer to him, keeping my gaze on a small bald spot on the back of his head. I couldn't think of him as a person. I had to think of him as a monster, otherwise I'd never go through with it.

The van slowed to take a sharp curve. I wrapped the chain around his neck, braced my feet against the back of the seat, and pulled with all my strength.

He gasped and pressed the gas pedal, letting go of the steering wheel. The van rocketed forward, taking the corner on two wheels.

My eyes widened as we sailed over an incline and rocketed down the slope of the mountain. I kept my hands tightly on the chain.

The van hit the bottom and rolled over twice, before coming to a stop on its side. I lay there, struggling to breath. My right leg throbbed. I stretched my hand down to find the gown torn and a piece of metal protruding from my thigh. Grasping the metal, I bit back a shriek and pulled it from my leg.

I moaned and lay still, assessing any further damage. My ribcage hurt, but not severely. Hopefully that meant bruised rather than broken. I turned my head to Death Glare.

He sat still, hanging half in and half out of the windshield. I wasn't going to stick around and find out whether he was dead. I needed to get out of the van and get to safety.

No easy task. My foot choice were heels or bare feet. I opted for bare feet. Since the gown was ripped up the side almost to my waist, movement was no longer hampered. I climbed over the front passenger seat and shimmied through the open window. I hadn't taken but two steps when I stopped.

I had to know his name. I might have killed the man. The least I could do is know his name.

I hopped to the ground. A quick rummage in his pockets and I located his wallet. David Wells. The man was dead. I sighed, knowing I might never know why he hated me so much and turned to glance up the mountain to where I knew the road was.

Climbing up would be impossible. I didn't have the strength, even with the adrenaline pumping through my veins. Blood ran down my leg in a steady stream. If I didn't put a tourniquet on, I'd bleed to death in that ravine.

I used a piece of glass to cut a strip from the bottom of my dress. I really loved this dress. A sob caught in my throat.

Taking a deep breath, I wrapped the strip of cloth around my leg and tied it as tight as I could. The pain took me to my knees. I rested for a moment, concentrating on taking deep, even breaths and blinking away the colored spots that danced in front of my eyes.

Once I could focus, I used the van to get to my feet. I had no idea which direction to go since the ground in front of me was too high to climb in a cast.

Wait. I stared down at David. *Please, have a cell phone.*

I patted him down like a cop frisking a prisoner. Nothing in his pants pocket or the pocket in the white chef-like jacket he wore. I hobbled to the van and peered inside. A cell phone lay on the floor, a foot out of reach.

The sobs escaped me. I'd have to climb back inside. I flopped on my belly on the windowsill and stretched. My fingers brushed the phone. I kicked my booted foot and inched forward, falling in a lump inside the van.

I grabbed the phone. No service. I struggled to stand and held the phone as high as I could. One bar.

I punched in Heath's number. "I need help."

"Oh, my God. I was so scared. Where are you?"

"I don't know. I'm bleeding, and I killed David."

"Who's David?"

"The man who took me." I scrunched into a ball and closed my eyes.

"How bad are you hurt?"

"We went over a cliff. I had to pull metal out of my leg. Can you come get me?" I started to cry harder.

"Keep the phone on. I'll have Seth trace it. I'm coming, baby. Hold on."

"The phone is about to die." I was afraid I was, too, but didn't want to voice the words. "I'm in the van."

"I'm co—" The phone died.

"No!" I stood again and dialed his number.

"What happened?"

"I don't have good reception. What if you can't find me? Heath, it's dark outside."

"I'm coming."

I could hear the sound of slamming doors, then the

roar of an engine over the phone. I guessed David had driven about twenty minutes from Shady Acres. If they could locate me via GPS, I didn't have long to wait.

I closed my eyes to the sound of Heath's soothing voice over the phone.

"Shelby!"

I fought to open my eyes and stared at Heath's silhouette in the moonlight. I reached for him and started crying again.

He took me under the arms and pulled me out of the van. I crumbled against him. He scooped me up and headed for a basket dangling under a helicopter. After securing me in, he caressed my face. "I'll meet you at the hospital."

I nodded and closed my eyes again. Really resolved this time to stop solving mysteries. Really and truly resolved.

Within minutes, I was taken from the basket and put into the chopper. We rose into the sky and sped away.

Once at the hospital, I was rushed inside where the nurses shook their heads at seeing me again and started cutting away my gown. They mumbled as if I weren't there and cleaned the wound on my leg.

The doctor arrived at the same time as Heath and Seth. I held my hand out to Heath.

He took it in his and sat in the chair next to the bed. "How are you doing?"

"I don't have a good leg or a nice formal gown anymore."

He gave a crooked smile. "The leg will heal, and I'll buy you a new gown."

"It won't be this gown." I sniffed. "I killed

someone."

"It was you or him."

Seth approached the bed. "Did you find out why you were targeted?"

"I didn't ask. I wrapped a chain around his neck and choked until the van went over the cliff."

Heath closed his eyes and shook his head. "You're lucky to be alive."

"I guess God doesn't want me yet." I winced as the doctor prodded my leg.

"It looks like a clean cut," he said. "Won't leave much of a scar." He told one of the nurses to stitch me up, then wrote on my chart. "Shelby Hart, you keep me in business." He gave a quick smile, then left.

I didn't find the humor in the situation at all.

The nurse numbed the wound and started stitching. I glanced at the black thread. Why was it always black? Why not a pretty color like pink or red?

"I'm getting very tired of this hospital," I said.

"I'm getting tired of seeing you in that bed." Heath kissed the palm of my hand, sending rivulets of warmth up my arm. "At least it's over now."

"Yeah, but we didn't get any answers."

"Maybe we'll find them when we dig into his background," Seth said. "I'll wait for you two in the waiting room."

Once I'd been stitched up and released, Seth drove us back to Shady Acres where all the residents waited for news on me in the dining room. Tears filled my eyes and I lifted my hand in a wave, leaning heavily on Heath's arm.

The room broke out into applause, this time for me. The only one not smiling and cheering was Susan. I felt bad about killing the man I thought might be her boyfriend, but Heath was right. It was him or me, and I was a survivor. Life had taught me that. I'd talk to her tomorrow.

"All right, folks." Heath held up a hand. "Now that we all know Shelby is going to be just fine, let's all go home and get some sleep. I know we need it. Thank you for your prayers and support."

He carried me to my cottage and straight to bed, bypassing Mom, Grandma, and Cheryl. "If they want to talk to you, they can come in here. You need to lie down."

"I love it when you're bossy." I smiled.

"No, you don't." He grinned and placed a gentle kiss on my lips. "I love you. I'm so glad I didn't lose you tonight."

"I'm pretty glad of that fact myself." I pulled him down for another kiss, feeling the pain medication the doctor had given me start to take effect. "I'll see you in the morning."

"Darn straight." He cupped my face. "I still think you should have spent the night in the hospital."

"No need. This is becoming a familiar occurrence to me." Unfortunately.

After reassuring my family and best friend that I was really fine, I drifted off to sleep dreaming of panel vans and clanking chains.

20

I slept in the next morning, waking to find a buttered croissant and fresh fruit on my nightstand. Every part of my body ached. My leg throbbed. My mouth felt full of cotton. But, I was alive and that was a good thing.

"No, you don't." Mom rushed into the room. "I can tell you're thinking of getting out of bed. That is not going to happen. You are going to lay there and rest for at least a day."

"I have a boot on one foot and a crutch to use for the leg. I'm fine to get around. No sense in being an invalid."

She planted fists on her hips. "Seriously? After what you went through, you can't take one day?" Tears welled in her eyes. "You had this entire community frightened out of their minds. The men all wanted to take up guns and track that man down.”

I grinned, my heart swelling. It was good to be loved. “All the more reason for me to see them.”

“Hog wash. You just don’t want to stay in bed. You waved at them last night.” She fluffed my pillows so I could sit up. “That will tide them over until tomorrow.”

I spotted Cheryl over Mom’s shoulder. “Help.”

She shook her head. “I learned a long time ago not to go against your mother.”

“What am I supposed to do all day?”

“Rest!” Mom made a sound in her throat and stormed from my room.

Feeling like a two year old having a temper tantrum, I pounded my fists against the mattress. “I don’t want to rest.”

“Take a pill,” Cheryl suggested, sitting in the one armchair in the room. “You’ll be asleep in thirty minutes.”

“Why did David Wells want to kill me?” The question would torment me for months if I didn’t get an answer.

She shrugged. “Seth will tell us if he finds out.”

Not good enough for me. I needed to know now. “Hand me my laptop, would you?”

“Your mom is going to kill both of us.” She left the room, returning a few minutes later with my computer. “I don’t know what you think you’re going to find.”

“Neither do I, but it will help me pass the time.”

She sat there and watched me surf the web before sighing and leaving me alone. Poor Cheryl. She hadn’t had much of a summer with me. No fun. Her only bright spot was meeting Seth.

I made a vow that we'd sit up late that night, watching chick flicks and eating too much. Just as we did when we were younger.

Ah, there you are. A tiny newspaper article hidden in cyberspace. David Wells had been arrested for assaulting a woman, then let go when she refused to press charges. That still didn't explain why he'd come after me.

"Hello, gorgeous." Heath leaned against the doorjamb.

"Hey, handsome." I lifted my face and pursed my lips. "You're the best thing I've seen all day."

He obliged by landing a long, sweet kiss on my lips. "I doubt you've seen much, stuck in that bed. What are you doing?"

"Trying to find out why David Wells hated me." I exhaled heavily. "No idea."

"Leave that to Seth and worry about getting healed." He sat in the chair Cheryl had vacated earlier. He hung his hands between his knees and stared at the floor. "I almost lost you, and I've been thinking long and hard about your chasing bad guys." He raised his head. "I don't want you to do it anymore."

While I'd come to the same conclusion, I didn't like being told what to do. I stared at my laptop. Even wounded, barely escaping death, I was still investigating. "I don't know if I can."

"If you don't, you'll die, and my life will never be the same." He stood and left without kissing me.

I set my laptop aside, laid back and cried myself to sleep.

When I woke, the moon had risen. Clouds danced across the sky. A shrouded figure stood framed in my window.

Wait. I bolted to a sitting position. "Cheryl!"

The figure left.

"Cheryl!"

"What?" She entered my room, hair mussed and face creased from her pillow. "Do you need your medication? A drink?"

"No. There was someone at the window."

She stuck her finger in her ear and scratched. "It's probably the drugs making you hallucinate."

"Will you at least check?" I flung the covers aside, fully prepared to get up and look for myself.

"Stay where you are hot pants. I'll look." She stepped up to the window and peered out. "No one there."

"Give me my crutch." I swung my legs over the bed, wincing as the stitches pulled.

"Where do you think you're going?"

"Outside. I know what I saw, Cheryl. I'm not hallucinating." Using the nightstand, I stretched until my hand wrapped around the crutch. "I'd appreciate it if you came with me to keep me from falling, but am I going."

"Your mother is going to kill me."

"Stop saying that. She won't do more than spit and sputter. You've been listening to that for years." I headed down the hall to the front door.

"Can I at least get some shoes on? You should wear a flip flop."

I glanced at my bare foot. The person was getting away! I slid my foot into a muddy flip flop next to the door and slowly opened the door, peering out. Every scary movie I'd ever watched ran through my head. I did not want to be a too-stupid-to-live-empty-headed girl.

I hobbled to the kitchen and pulled a hammer from the junk drawer. Cheryl joined me, clutching a flashlight and my gun. We were as ready as we could be.

Opening the front door wide, we stepped outside, weapons held in front of us, and shuffled around the corner of the cottage. No boogeyman to greet us. No shrouded figure.

"Shine the light under my window." I bet a dime to a doughnut we'd find size eight and a half footprints.

She did as I asked, illuminating a fresh print. "David Wells has a girlfriend or a really tiny footed partner."

I agreed. The mystery, or the danger, wasn't over yet. "Let's get inside before they come back."

"They won't come back." Cheryl stomped behind me. "The partner that's left only wants to scare you. Wells was the take charge one. I wish they'd come back." She waved my gun. "I really do."

"Put that away before you shoot someone. Like…hey, Leroy!"

Our resident vampire turned and came toward us.

Cheryl stepped behind me. "What if he's the bad guy?"

"Don't be ridiculous."

Leroy gave a thin-lipped smile. "What are you two up to so late at night?"

"Did you see a hooded figure wandering around?" I eyed the jacket he wore.

"Again?" He shook his head. "You're the first two I've seen in over an hour. I saw Ted leaving your

Grandmother's place, and Madeline Cross doing the walk of shame from Dean Roof's place, but no one else." He grinned. "Yes, I wander everywhere, even the rooms upstairs."

The person was a ghost, a phantom that appeared and disappeared at will. Eventually, they'd have to confront me, and I'd be ready.

~

The next morning, I limped and clunked and dragged myself to breakfast. No more staying in bed all day where anyone could walk in and catch me alone. I intended to make sure I had someone with me at all times.

I spotted Heath and Seth already seated and rushed to them. Well, as fast as someone wearing a boot with stitches could move using a crutch.

"They came back. The size eight and a half came back last night. Cheryl and I confirmed by seeing a fresh print outside my window." I sat down and crossed my arms. "I wasn't even snooping." I sent Heath a 'look'. "I was sleeping. Actually, I had just woken up."

They both stared at me as if I'd turned blue. "Well? Aren't either of you going to say anything?"

Cheryl plopped a muddy gym shoe on the table. "Guess who wears a size eight and a half and quit this morning?"

Seth groaned. "We talked about this."

"What? About me not helping Shelby? She can't go snooping around all crippled like she is." Cheryl grinned.

"Aren't you going to tell us who?" I stared at the shoe.

"Susan Hall."

I remembered the glares when I'd returned after killing David. It all made sense. Except, she was gone now. "Any idea where she might have gone? I know she lived in one of the servant's cottages."

Seth got up from the table, returning a few minutes later with the type of white bag cooks sometimes packed lunches in. He picked up the shoe with the tips of his forefinger and thumb and dropped it into the bag. "I'll take this to the station. Please, stay out of trouble until I return." He rushed out the door.

"I don't think he knows who he is talking to," Heath said.

Poor Heath. I really did cause him headaches.

"What's wrong, dear?" Grandma patted Heath's shoulder as she sat down. "What has Shelby done now?"

"Seriously? Why does his long face always have to do with me?" I frowned, reaching for my glass of orange juice.

"Well, is it?" She raised her eyebrows.

"I had another visitor last night. Cheryl found out that Susan wears the right size shoe days ago, and just discovered that she quit this morning."

"Why do I miss all the good stuff?" Grandma tossed a napkin on the table and glared at Ted who sat next to her.

"What did I do?"

"Kept me awake too late so that I slept in and missed all the fun."

I could have told her that having Ted sleep over was what she deserved. But, Grandma was Grandma, and never made excuses for her actions. I loved her despite her wayward, drinking ways. Unfortunately, she remained an embarrassment to my straight-laced mother, who, as we spoke, marched toward us with a grim look on her face. Wait. She was glaring at me.

"Why are you out of bed?" She plunked a plate of food in front of me. "I went to feed you and found the place empty and Seth digging in the dirt."

She paled as Cheryl explained what had happened. "I thought it was over." Mom sagged into a seat.

"I think we all did."

"I'll be moving in with you and Cheryl tonight. There is safety in numbers."

Not to be outdone, Grandma raised her hand. "Me, too. I'll sleep with Cheryl. Sue Ellen can sleep with Shelby. Heath, you get the couch."

He shot her a look. "Why would I want to spend the night with you four?"

Grandma playfully slapped his arm. "It'll be fun! Wine, popcorn, Truth or Dare. We'll have a slumber party while we wait for a killer to show up."

21

*H*eath chose not to come to our slumber party. I couldn't blame him, not really. What man in his right mind, unless he still possessed a high school mentality, wanted to hang out with women who wore green clay masks on their face and painted each other's nails?

"I still think he should have come," Grandma said, pouring wine into a glass. "We need a man here to protect us."

"We have two guns and a Tazer. Besides, it's a slumber party. Only killers in B-Horror movies crash those." I propped my feet on the coffee table.

"That's true," she said, nodding. "And, we're on the alert. Those silly bimbos in the movies are always taken unawares."

Mom stared wide-eyed at each of us. "We got

together tonight in the hopes of drawing out the killer? Isn't Susan the killer? Oh, what am I doing here?"

"Hanging out with us," Cheryl said. "Susan isn't going to be stupid enough to come here. You're safe." She rubbed her hands together. "What movie are we going to watch? A scary murder movie or a tear-jerker?"

Of course, Grandma wanted scary and Mom wanted tear-jerker. Cheryl voted scary. That left me to either break the tie or vote with the majority. I glanced at the clock. Only eight p.m. "Let's watch scary, then tear jerker, so we can actually sleep."

"Fine." Mom slammed back in her chair. "But, we're keeping a light on."

Cheryl chose a movie about a deaf woman terrorized by a stranger. Even I clutched a pillow to my chest throughout the movie, only peering over the top when I shouted something stupid, like "Run." She couldn't have heard me even if she was standing right next to me.

Mom got up at every scary part, which was most of the movie, and hid in the bathroom. Each time, she turned on every light between here and there.

My cell phone rang as the killer struggled with a male victim putting up a fight. I shrieked and grabbed it. "Hello." I motioned for Cheryl to pause the movie.

"What's wrong?" Heath asked.

"Nothing. We're watching a scary movie and the phone startled me. What's up?"

"Just checking on you ladies. The lights keep going on and off."

"That's Mom running to the bathroom every two seconds because she's scared."

He laughed. "Okay. I'll talk to you in the morning."

We hung up and Cheryl pressed play on the remote. For the next fifteen minutes, we sat on the edges of our seats as this brave deaf woman gave the killer his justice.

"Oh, my," Grandma said. "That's way more scary than those horror flicks with Jason and Michael. This one could really happen." She cut a quick glance to the window.

"This is why I don't like scary movies," Mom said. "Her imagination is going to run into overtime. She'll see bad guys behind every bush. She'll drive me insane."

The lights went out. We all screamed and glanced at the front door.

Thunder boomed. I relaxed. Nothing more than a storm. "I'll get the flashlights."

Using my cell phone to see by, I went to the kitchen and dug out the two tiny flashlights I owned. I clicked one on to make sure it worked, and shined it at the window. The beam illuminated the shape of a person standing on the other side of the sheers I used as curtains.

Mom screamed. Grandma ran down the hall. Cheryl grabbed the nearest lamp—as a weapon, I guessed.

My first instinct was to dash outside, but wearing a boot and having stitches in my leg didn't allow me to dash anywhere. "Go catch her!"

Cheryl looked at me as if I were nuts. "Absolutely not. People have died."

"For crying out loud." I limped for the door.

Mom planted herself in front of me. "You are not going out there. You're in no condition to defend yourself."

"She's going to get away." I tried to squeeze past her. Mom didn't budge. She was really strong when she wanted to be. Right now, she really wanted to be.

Someone knocked on the door.

We froze.

Grandma peered around the corner of the bedroom. "Do killers knock?"

"Not usually." With my heart beating in my throat, I parted the sheers, and smiled. Heath stood on the stoop, a pillow and blanket in hand.

Just as I went to let the curtains fall into place, a black clothed figure hit him over the head with a rock, then raced away. Heath groaned and fell to his knees. Mom or not, I yanked open the front door and knelt next to Heath.

"Are you all right?" I tried to see the back of his head in the dark.

"Hold this." He shoved the bedding into my arms, got to his feet, and sprinted in the direction the assailant had gone.

"Grandma, call—"

"Already dialing Teddy's number."

"I'm calling Seth," Cheryl said.

"I'll get an ice pack," Mom called out.

While they did something constructive, I stood there, clutching the pillow and blanket, and stared into the night waiting for Heath to return safely. As the minutes ticked by, my anxiety grew.

Susan, if it really was her in the black clothes, liked to play games. I was tired of playing. The person responsible for the poisoning needed to be locked up. I may have said I wasn't going to do anymore investigations, but I also wasn't happy about sitting back and doing nothing while someone terrorized my family and friends. No, it was getting to be time for a show down.

Heath came back the same time Seth and Teddy barged up the walkway. "She got away."

"She?" Seth asked. "Are you sure it was a woman that hit you?"

"Unless a man was wearing a bra, yes. This woman had breasts. I got a clear look at her profile. Then, she just disappeared."

I gasped. "The tunnels." I was no way going down there ever again. Not after what happened a few months ago.

"I boarded those up," Teddy said.

"Anyone with a hammer could rip off the boards," Heath explained. "Let's get inside where we're not in the open."

We all gathered in my tiny living room and perched on any surface we could. Naturally, we all started talking at once, until Ted put his fingers to his lips and let loose a shrill whistle. "Shelby, you saw what happened. Talk."

"We had just finished watching a scary movie. We saw a shadowy figure on the front porch. When I looked out, I saw that it was Heath. Then, someone dressed in black ran up behind him and bashed him over the head with a rock. Did anyone pick up the rock?"

Seth shook his head. "I'll get it. Heath, are you bleeding?"

"No, just a bump. I have a headache, but nothing more."

I scooted closer to him on the couch. "Then, Heath took off after the person."

"They got away," he said.

Seth sighed. "I'll go get the rock." He returned a few minutes later with a bulging bag. "I doubt they'll find any prints, but I'll take this to the station. I'm getting real tired of this person." He left and Cheryl locked the door.

"I go back to work on Monday," she said. "Do you think we can wrap this up in two days? I don't want to miss the ending."

"Sometimes the finale isn't something you want to experience," I said. "But, we do need a plan. We can't keep looking over our shoulders."

"I seriously think David Wells was the killer," Ted said. "Susan, if it is Susan, is the partner. I could be wrong, but she doesn't seem as daring as Wells."

"Why stick around?" I rolled my head on my shoulders. "With David dead, she could disappear."

"Obviously, whatever reason she had for offing Lloyd Dane hasn't been resolved." Ted gave Grandma a quick kiss. "See you in the morning. I don't think it wise for any of you to go anywhere alone. Not until this person is caught."

I agreed. So much for a fun slumber party. "I'm beat. Heath, the sofa is all yours. Grandma, you're sleeping with Cheryl. Mom, you're with me."

"Cheryl snores." Grandma frowned. "Loudly."

"Wear earplugs." I was too tired to argue. I kissed Heath goodnight and shuffled to bed.

~

Having decided the next morning to keep last night's events a secret from the other residents, we filled our plates from the breakfast buffet and carried our food back to my place. We were going to set a trap. If there was no we, then I would set one myself.

With plates balanced on knees, we ate, skirting around Heath's attack. It wasn't until we'd stacked the empty plates that I finally spoke. "Now what?"

"Well," Ted straightened in his chair. "This person has a bone to pick with you for some reason. I say we use you as bait."

"No," Heath said, around the rim of his glass.

"Not my Shelby," Mom said, shaking her head.

"If not me," I fixed stern glances on them, "then who? I'm the one they're stalking."

"But you're injured and can't run away." Mom gave an emphatic nod. "I'll do it. I'll be the worm on the hook."

I shook my head. "I appreciate the gesture, but it won't work. This person has nothing against you." I didn't know what they had against me either, but that was beside the point.

Seth barged into my cottage without knocking, and glared. "Why isn't this door locked?"

I grinned. "How else would you get in uninvited?"

"Not funny." He pulled up a kitchen chair. "I've got some interesting news, if you want to hear."

We all leaned forward.

"Lloyd Duncan is Susan Hall's uncle. He was married to her mother. Now," he raised a hand, "this is where it gets very interesting. I've done some digging after reading that diary you found. It seems that another cousin, is none other than our dear mayor. We found the beginnings of a book detailing the illegal alcohol trade that their family was into years ago. My reasoning is that Lloyd was killed to keep this story from being circulated."

"So the mayor is the bad guy?" I cocked my head. "Do you think he's putting Susan up to this?"

"If it is Susan. That's only speculation. Anyway, I have a meeting with our esteemed mayor in an hour. I'm not a cop who usually divulges information on an ongoing case, but since this person has targeted you, Shelby, I thought you might want to know."

"I appreciate that. Now, how do we go about luring the responsible person out of hiding?" I didn't understand the reasoning behind keeping ages old information secret, but sometimes pride was a powerful thing.

"Don't do anything stupid," he said, standing. "We're getting close. No need for you to do anything."

Ted laughed. "That's like giving Shelby the go-ahead."

"Ha ha." But, Ted was right. I had no intentions of sitting back and doing nothing. Today was Saturday. Cheryl left soon to return to teaching. I paused in my thinking. By stalling, she'd leave and be out of danger. I'd let the weekend go without snooping, and resume on Monday, alone.

22

I managed to use the pain of my stitches as an excuse to keep Cheryl's snooping at bay. On Monday morning, I gave her a hug, waved her off, and went to the only place I might find a bit of privacy…the green house.

It wasn't the most peaceful place on the grounds since I'd found a dead body there on my first day of employment. But, it was that reason that kept most of the residents away.

I sat on a crate of gardening tools and tried to formulate a plan. The only thing I could think of was to make plenty of opportunities to be taken. An idea that held little appeal. After a while, I considered going into the tunnels, and shuddered. Only a tornado would get me down into the dark again.

I ran over what I knew. The mayor, Lloyd Duncan,

and Susan were all related to the long time ago writer of the diary. They had made illegal moonshine. Someone, apparently wanted to prevent the story from being told. A bit extreme, to resort to murder, but I guessed they thought it important enough.

Who, besides me, at Shady Acres knew enough about poisonous plants to have someone unsuspectedly ingest some? I really, really needed to get inside people's homes. How? With a boot and a wounded leg, I moved like a ninety-year-old woman. If I were to get caught, that would be the end.

"What's wrong?" Heath entered the building and leaned against the work station.

"You won't like it."

"Probably not, but tell me anyway."

"I need to find out who knows poisonous foliage. In order to do that, I need to snoop more in people's cabins." I turned my head, not wanting to see the disappointment in his eyes.

"Something like this?" He handed me a small paperback.

I glanced into his smiling face. "Exactly!" The title was Poisonous Plants and How to Use Them. "Where did you find this?"

"Alice had me cleaning out Susan's room. I found it between the mattresses."

"I guess this tells us she's the culprit. Probably had David do her dirty work while she runs around annoying me." I flipped through the pages, finding the plants used on Lloyd and Alice. Now, to lure Susan out of hiding.

God, help me know what to do. The thought froze me. I hadn't talked to God since my father died. Why would He help me out of a situation I'd gotten myself into? A situation I had no business being a part of?

"I don't know what to do." I sighed.

"Give the book to Seth." Heath placed a hand on my shoulder. "You've done all you could. We've actually uncovered more information than the police. You should be proud."

I was, really. Even more so at Heath's words. But, I hated to start something I couldn't finish. "I'd better get to work. I've some weeding to do in the planters near the parking lot."

"I'll come with you. We aren't supposed to go anywhere alone." He put a hand to his head. "I'm not looking to get hit again."

"You poor baby." I took his hand and got to my feet. "I'm glad it wasn't worse."

"Me, too." He pulled me close and kissed me. "We're overdue for a date. The party you threw your grandmother didn't turn out quite the way I'd hoped."

I laughed. "Sure, you can come along. I'll let you do all the work while I recline back like a lady of leisure." As I turned to leave, a potted plant caught my eye.

Closer inspection revealed the plant to be fool's parsley. The culprit that killed Lloyd. How many of these plants were scattered around the grounds?

"What is that?" Heath peered over my shoulder.

"The murder weapon, is my guess. Susan has this stuff planted everywhere for easy access. We'll give this to Seth, too." I hefted the plant in my arms and followed Heath to the front of the complex.

He called Seth and we settled down to wait. While we did, I eyed the plants that needed pruning and weeding. Since Heath could kneel easy enough, it wouldn't take him long. I pointed out what needed doing and headed inside to talk with Mom.

She was bent over her computer peering intently at her computer screen. "Look at this," she said, not looking up.

I moved to her side of the desk. It was a small news article on a Susan Tollson Hall. She'd been arrested for shoplifting ten years prior, of all things, books on the prohibition. "One more strike to show she's our guilty person."

"I had an idea." Mom sat back and crossed her arms. "I hate your snooping, but know you won't stop until this over. What if you write a press release saying you're going to write a book on prohibition in Boonesville? You don't have to put any names in the article, but it should be enough that Susan will stop playing games and confront you."

"Mom, you're a genius." I gave her a big hug. "Let's do it."

"I have a friend who works for the paper. She'll make sure the article gets in." She pulled up a blank document and started typing.

We didn't notice Seth leaning over the counter until he cleared his throat loudly.

"Gracious, Seth." Mom put a hand to her throat. "You scared me."

"My apologies. What are the two of you engrossed in?"

"Nothing." Mom minimized her screen and pasted on a smile. "How may I help you?"

He narrowed his eyes. "Just letting Shelby know I took the plant and the book. We have an APB out on

Susan Hall. We should have her in custody soon."

"Aren't you the optimistic one?" Mom patted his hand. "You go do that. I have work to do."

It was clear from the look on his face that he knew we were up to something, but wisely held his tongue. I did hear him mutter something about, "Poor Heath," as he went out the door.

It wasn't the first time someone had pity on my boyfriend.

Mom had an article typed in ten minutes. "Send." She pressed a button on the keyboard and rubbed her hands together. "Now, make sure you have your gun and your Tazer on you at all times. I'm serious, Shelby."

"Understood. I'll go get them now." I had a shoulder pouch I could carry them in. "Thanks again, Mom. Tell Heath where I've gone if he finishes before I return, okay?"

I expected something to happen as I made my way to my cottage. Every few steps, I glanced over my shoulder, certain I could feel someone's stare. When I reached my destination, I hurried inside and locked the door, then headed for my bedroom closet where I'd stashed the weapons in a box on the top shelf.

I stretched and retrieved the box as the closet door slammed and I found myself in total darkness. Then, the sound of something heavy being slid in front of the door. I should have checked to make sure I was alone. This time, I'd outsmarted Susan. I fished my cell phone from my pocket and dialed Heath.

"Someone locked me in my closet."

"I'll be right there."

It took him five minutes. When he released me, he

handed me a sheet of paper on which was printed the words, "Go away and never come back."

I rolled my eyes. Not a very threatening note in my opinion. She didn't add "or else". I wasn't worried. The games would come to an end with tomorrow's paper.

~

Heath didn't speak to me the rest of the afternoon or at supper. At least, not until he'd berated me for not letting an hour go by before I went off on my own.

I tried explaining that I needed my weapons, Mom's orders, but he wouldn't listen. So, I picked at my salad like a reprimanded child and tried to figure out how I was going to pass the time while I waited for a killer to find me.

"Why are you not eating?" Joyce stood next to my chair. "I personally tested every tray of food. No poison."

"It's not that." I knew Joyce now watched over her kitchen like a fanatic. "I'm not hungry."

"Eat. Otherwise, you waste my time." She turned to leave.

"Wait."

"What?"

"You wouldn't happen to have heard from Susan?"

"Sure. She picked up her last check today. Why?"

My shoulders slumped. "Didn't anyone tell you she's the primary suspect in a murder investigation?"

Joyce's eyes widened. "No. If I had known, I would have locked her in the freezer until the police came. Will they arrest me?"

I shook my head. "You didn't know. Is there any way you can get her to come back? Tell her you shorted her check or something?"

"Yes, I can do that. Let me see if she'll answer the phone. If she does, I'll tell her to come in tomorrow, early, before the breakfast rush. That way, she won't expect anything. I will let you know." She hurried to the kitchen.

"Smart thinking," Heath said.

"Now, you're talking to me?"

"Don't be that way, Shelby. If you don't stay by my side, I can't protect you." He tapped my nose with his forefinger. "I worry about you. Don't be angry with me for that."

"I'm not. I completely understand. I don't want you in harm's way either. Having you next to me defeats that purpose."

"Are we interrupting anything?" Grandma and Ted sat across from us. "What's the latest in the games?"

I told them of being locked in the closet and how Mom put an article in the paper.

"Now, you'll have to write that book, Shelby." Grandma shook her head. "Otherwise, folks will be asking on a regular basis why it isn't finished yet."

"I'll tell them the truth." A writer, I wasn't.

She shrugged. "Maybe I'll write it. I need a hobby."

Good. Maybe writing would keep her out of trouble.

Ted drummed his fingers on the table. "Where is Sue Ellen?"

We glanced around the room. I hadn't seen her since the afternoon when she'd come up with her brilliant plan.

My heart skipped a beat as I fished my cell phone from my pocket. No answer, so I left her a voice mail.

I'd try again in five minutes. If no response, Seth would be the next person I called.

My anxiety grew as the seconds ticked by.

Worry lines grew around Grandma's eyes. "My daughter isn't made of tough enough stuff to deal with this. Go find her, Teddy."

He stood and caressed Grandma's cheek. "I will."

"Call her again, Shelby," Grandma said, turning back to me.

I nodded and pressed Mom's number. Again, no answer. "Does she have a GPS tracker?"

"Not that I know of. I've never had a reason to keep tabs on her before. She's always been reliable."

"Heath, I'm scared. What if Susan found out what Mom was up to?" I stared up at him.

"How could she have?" He pulled me into his lap, not caring about the disapproving looks of a few of the older women. He put me on my feet. "Let's get out of here. Maybe she had an appointment she didn't tell you about. Keep calling her phone."

Birdie, one of the more colorful characters of the community, bustled toward us like a sparrow, her gaze darting here and there. "Shelby!" She folded her hands over her chest. "I have bad news. Really bad news."

"Just tell me." I wanted to shake her. I didn't have time to guess what she wanted to say.

"Well, you know I have a talent for eavesdropping."

"Yes?"

"So, I know everyone here is looking for Susan Hall."

"Birdie, please!"

Just as my cell phone rang with my mother's

number, Birdie said, "That evil woman shoved your mother into the trunk of a car."

23

I gave Birdie a crazy look, and pressed answer on my phone. "Mom?"

"That crazy woman shoved mc into her car. I swear, Shelby, I've got bruises the size of dinner plates."

My heart plummeted. "Where are you?"

"Some cabin in the…oops. I'm supposed to stick to the facts. Although, that's an important fact in my book." She sighed. "If you want me back a live, you have to bring the manuscript and yourself. Details to follow."

"But, I don't have a manu—" The phone went dead. I locked gazes with Heath. "Susan has my mother in a cabin somewhere. I have to start writing a book, right now." I set off for my cottage, an entourage trailing after me.

"Shelby, wait." Heath grabbed my arm and spun me around to face him. "Don't go off half-cocked. What do you mean you have to write a book?"

I explained Mom's crazy idea. "There must be a snitch at the newspaper, because there is no way Susan could have read the article yet."

Grandma gasped. "I'll help you. It doesn't have to be good. Just something to make that woman think we've turned it over."

"Just tell her you don't have it." Heath glanced from me to her. "Anyone with half a brain would know you would keep a backup of a manuscript."

Good point. Tears welled in my eyes. "I don't know what to do."

"I do." Birdie raised her hand. "Susan's family has a hunting cabin on the mountain. I'd bet my pink hair that's where she's holding your mother. Now, I'm too old to go gallivanting up there, but I can draw you a map. I spent a lot of time there in my youth."

I hugged her. "You're a marvel."

"It's the least I can do for you catching Mabel's killer." She grinned. "Besides, Sue Ellen is the best receptionist we've ever had. You go get your mother."

Ted slid his cell phone into his pocket. "Seth is on his way. He said to meet us at Shelby's cabin."

Everything in me wanted to barge up the mountain. Experience taught me that wasn't the wisest course of action. I unlocked my cottage door and ushered everyone inside.

Birdie tore a sheet of paper off a notepad I kept next to the fridge and drew a crude map. "There's a lot of tree coverage, so you should be able to sneak up easily enough."

"Thank you." I hugged her again and sent her on her way. I loved the little woman, but her loose lips would alert anyone for fifty miles around as to what we were planning.

"It'll be all right." Heath gathered me in his arms. "We'll get her back."

I nodded, my nose pressing into his chest. "I really think it's time to start praying."

"If God doesn't mind a smart-mouthed, wine drinking granny, then I'm game." Grandma held out her hands. "Come on. Prayer circle."

We gathered around and held hands and prayed silently, no one comfortable enough with the unfamiliar act to pray out loud. When we'd finished, Grandma made tea while the rest of us waited for Seth.

He arrived ten minutes later.

I jumped to feet. "What do we do?"

"Wait for the next call."

I groaned and plopped back to the sofa. Waiting was not one of my talents.

When the phone did ring, we all jumped as if a shot had gone off. I grabbed my phone. "Yeah?"

"Okay," Mom said. "Susan, you were right about her being the culprit, said to bring what you have to the family cabin…she said you could figure it out…in two hour's time. Oh, and if you don't come alone, she'll make me drink poison Kool Aid. She isn't very creative, is she?" Mom sighed. "Fine. She said to stop the chit chat. See you in two hours." Click.

I relayed the message to the others. "I'm going alone. I'll shove my gun down my pants and save Mom myself. I'm not taking any chances."

Grandma shook her head. "That's not a wise choice, dear. You'll shoot off…well, your girly parts. You aren't the most graceful person. I'll have to go with you. I'm sure she only means not to bring the men."

Seth took a deep breath and stared at the wall across from us from several minutes before speaking, "I don't want to take the chance with your mother, either. We'll send you two in, with Shelby wearing a wire. Law enforcement will hide in the woods. At the first sound that things are headed south, we'll have to come in." He switched his gaze to me. The hard glint in his eyes told me this was the plan and I could take it or leave it.

I chose to take it. "Sounds good. Get me wired."

Since there wasn't a female officer to help, he explained what I needed to do and sent me to the bathroom with a small microphone and tape. Not wanting the wire to slip and reveal its presence, I used several strips of the sticky tape and adhered it to my skin.

"I'm ready," I said, joining the others back in the living room.

"I don't like this. None of it makes any sense," Heath said. "Why has Susan chosen you?"

"I guess we'll find out soon enough." Grandma was right about the gun, but I did slip the Tazer into the waistband of my underpants and pulled my shirt down to cover it.

Seth herded us to a black SUV, having Grandma and me sit in the back. "I'm going to drive you as far as the end of the road leading up the mountain. You'll have to walk quite a ways up hill. Since there's a time limit, no dawdling."

Grandma grabbed my hand and squeezed. "That's my baby up there. I won't slow you down."

"I know you won't." I squeezed back and kept a tight grip on her hand while Seth drove the forty-five minutes to where the road forked off from the highway. No one spoke, each lost in their dark thoughts.

Why had Susan targeted me? It could be as simple as the fact that I'd identified how Lloyd had died and fished a book of poison out of the dumpster. Since this was the third time I'd gotten involved in solving a murder, it made a lot of sense.

Then, as I continued to investigate, saving Alice by being in the right place at the right time, snooping through cottages and rental rooms, Susan would have known it was only a matter of time before I got lucky and pinned the poisonings on her. Add in the fact she thought I was going to take up the book where Lloyd left off, and she most likely thought I was a real threat. I needed to show her that I wasn't.

"What are you thinking?" Grandma whispered, leaning close.

"That Susan targeting me was by accident. I simply got in the way, like Mom. I won't have an idea for us getting away until we get there." I eyed the boot on my foot. Running wasn't an easy option, but I'd do it if I had to.

"This is it." Seth pulled onto the shoulder of the highway. "Keep the mic on at all times. Oh, and walk fast. You have to just a little over an hour."

Grandma and I shoved our doors open. Heath climbed from the front passenger seat and grabbed me in a bone-crushing hug. "Be careful. I don't want to live in a world that doesn't include Shelby Hart."

I smiled into his face. "You won't have to. I'll meet you up the hill." I studied every line and angle of his face, sincerely hoping I'd see him again. I grabbed a backpack from the floorboard, glanced at Heath again as I shrugged into it, then squared my shoulders. "Let's do this."

Hand-in-hand, Grandma and I started up the winding mountain road. "We turn left at the…is that supposed to be a tree split in half?"

I peered at the map. "Looks like it, but we've a ways to go. That looks like it's halfway up." I really hoped Birdie's map skills were up to par.

A dark cloud shrouded the sun, making the day seem dreary and menacing. Already frightened, the sun hiding seemed like a bad omen.

"At least it isn't hot," Grandma said, as if she could read my mind. "Autumn can still be warm and we are hiking up a steep hill." She stopped and bent over, placing her hands on her thighs to take in deep breaths. After a few seconds, she straightened and nodded. "I'm ready."

"Maybe you should stay behind. I don't want you having a heart attack."

She grinned. "If you can do this with a boot, I can do this. Besides, I plan on having a fake heart attack to play on whatever mercy Susan might have. Sweating and heavy breathing will only help my play acting."

"It might also cause the guys to storm in with guns blazing."

"I already told Teddy my plan."

We came to a tree that looked as if it had been struck by lightning and split in half. A dirt road turned off from the one we walked. We made the turn and kept walking. A quick glance at the time on my cell phone showed we had a little under half an hour to reach our destination. I prayed we were headed in the right direction.

"According to the map, we should be almost there." Grandma folded the paper and stuck it under her bra strap. "What?" She raised her eyebrows. "There aren't any pockets in these leggings. They're new. Do you like them?" She stuck out one multi-colored, swirled leg. "I bet I stick out from the foliage in these."

"Not exactly a good thing when we run and have to hide."

"No worries. I wore a green blouse. I'll shed the leggings. The blouse is long enough to cover my behind."

Lord, have mercy.

The road hadn't been traveled in a while and rocks and weeds prevented me from traveling as fast as I'd like. Each time I stumbled, I worried about our deadline.

"What flavor of Kool Aid do you think she has?"

I cut her a sharp look. "Seriously?"

"Well, if we lose this fight, I prefer cherry as my last drink. Actually, wine would be best, but I doubt she has any."

I laughed, startling a black bird from a tree. "If I have to do this with anyone, I'm glad it's you."

"Ditto, girl." Grandma grinned and hooked her arm with mine. "What an adventure we've had since moving to Shady Acres."

An understatement for sure. "I once thought teaching third grade was adventurous."

"No way. Kids are fun, but not as exhilarating as escaping the clutches of a killer. We should have brought water. I'm dying of thirst."

I handed her a bottle from my pack. "We'll have to share. I'm going to stash this pack of food and water," plus my gun, "in the woods. We'll grab it when we get free."

"That's my girl. Always thinking ahead."

I spotted a cabin through the trees and shed the backpack. I shoved it under a nearby bush and kicked leaves over the camouflage fabric. Not that I expected Susan to think I'd brought one, but just in case, I didn't want it found.

With eyes glued straight ahead, I led the way into a small clearing. Smoke curled from a rock fireplace. The cabin, while small, was very well kept. Under different circumstances, I wouldn't have minded spending a week there.

"Ready?" I glanced at Grandma.

"I was born ready. What do we do now?"

"We announce ourselves and save my mom."

24

I turned on the mic and called out, "Hello!"

"That sounds too friendly," Grandma said, frowning. "Hey! We're here. Come on out!"

"Don't antagonize her." Maybe bringing Grandma hadn't been a good idea after all.

"Put your hands up!" Susan's voice rang out an open window. "I told you to come alone, Shelby."

We put our hands up.

"I'm an old lady come to fetch my daughter." Grandma clenched her fists. "Try and get rid of me."

"Too late for that now. Come on, nice and slow."

We gave each other a quick glance, and walked slowly toward the house. When no shots rang out, we climbed the three steps to the porch.

Susan yanked open the front door. "Hurry up.

Stand against the wall.”

We did as we were told.

Mom sat on a faded sofa, sipping a glass of what looked like tea. It surprised me that she would drink anything offered by a person who poisoned those she wanted to get rid of.

“Spread your arms and legs.” Susan pointed a Glock at my head. “Come on.”

Sighing, I did, knowing what was coming next.

Susan ran her hands over my body, then ripped my tee shirt over my head. “I knew it.” She yanked the mic from my skin.

“Ow!” She had to have taken skin with it, I’d used so much tape to secure the tiny recording device.

She ground it under her heel, then repeated the patting down on Grandma while I put my shirt back on. “At least you’re clean. Have a seat on the sofa.” Once we had, she continued, “Now, where’s the manuscript.”

“I don’t have one. It was only an idea that hadn’t gotten off the ground.” I glanced at Mom, praying she’d told the same story.

“Now, it never will. Are y’all thirsty? I made sweat tea.”

“Go ahead,” Mom said. “I’ve been drinking it all day and I’m still breathing.”

“What if it’s a slow acting poison?” Grandma said, peering into her glass.

“For crying out loud. I have a gun now. Why would I poison my favorite drink?” Susan stomped to a small kitchen area in the corner. “Come watch me, if you’re so untrusting.”

I still didn’t trust her. “Do you have any unopened bottles of water?”

"Don't try my patience, Shelby. It your fault we're all here. Now, I have to figure out what to do with the three of you."

"Actually," Mom held up a finger. "The book idea was mine."

"A real pity, Sue Ellen. I've grown to like you over the last few hours. You don't whine or complain. I thought we might actually be friends, under different circumstances."

"I'm a great friend," Grandma said. "Open to adventures of all kinds."

"Good. Then you must be having a blast." With all the graciousness of an unwilling host, she plunked two glasses of iced tea in front of us, then sat in an armchair. In one hand, she still clutched her weapon, in the other, her tea. "So, how long do we have before the cavalry shows up? Crushing the mic was probably not the smartest thing I've ever done."

Neither was taking three people hostage, but I held my tongue. "Half an hour, maybe."

She pressed her lips together. "Well, drink up. We've got to go. I've got a van parked in the back."

I declined to take a sip of the tea, despite Mom and Grandma drinking their's. Once they'd finished, Susan ushered us through a door next to the kitchen. A white panel van sat next to a dilapidated shed. Why was it always a panel van the bad guys used?

"How are you going to retrieve your backpack?" Grandma whispered, climbing into the back.

"I have no idea, but I'll think of something." I had to. Our lives depended on us, at least me, getting free and retrieving my gun. Seeing my opportunity, I clapped Grandma on the shoulder. "Be careful. Watch for me."

As Susan climbed into the driver's seat, I bolted for the woods, fully expecting a bullet in the back. When one didn't come, I kept running, skirting the house. I ducked as the van stopped on the other side of the bushes where I hunkered down.

The passenger window rolled down. "I know you can hear me, Shelby. Running will not accomplish anything. Maybe you'll never see these two again. What do you think about that?" She roared away, spraying gravel over my head.

She had a good point. I shed the boot and raced for the pack. Grabbing it on the run, I took off through the trees toward a sharp curve I knew she would have to slow down for. Every once in a while, I caught a glimpse of the van through the branches.

I fumbled for the gun as I ran. When the van slowed rounding the curve, I aimed and pulled the trigger. My third shot took out the rear tire.

The van fishtailed, before slamming into a tree.

I stood in horror, believing I may have killed my family. Then, the sliding panel opened and Mom and Grandma staggered out and ran in my direction.

"Get down," I hissed. Thank you, God, for sparing them. "Where's Susan?"

"Her head hit the steering wheel. She must be out cold," Grandma said. "Let's boogie while we still can. Great plan, by the way."

"Risky," Mom said. "We could have been killed."

"I didn't think of that until the van crashed."

"Some things you need to think of before acting."

I shrugged. The relief of seeing them free from a woman who clearly didn't have her full mental capabilities filled me with joy.

"Where's your boot?" Mom put her hands on her hips.

"I couldn't run with it. I'll worry about that later. Let's go." I led them away from the road. If I'd paid attention while walking from the highway, we should reach it in a little shorter time than it had taken to get to the cabin.

While we fought thick underbrush, I dug my cell phone from the pack and called Heath. "We're free."

"Thank God. Where are you?"

"Uh, in the woods. The van we escaped from is on the road. No idea if Susan is still inside."

"Stay where you are. We'll find you."

Which sounded like an excellent idea, until Susan shouted my name from somewhere to our left. "Can't. She's coming, and she sounds very upset." With Mom and Grandma following, we ducked and squeezed into the thicket.

"You should have left well enough alone, Shelby," Susan said.

I motioned for Mom and Grandma to be still and quiet. I put a finger to my lips, then pointed to the road.

"I wouldn't have killed you. My plan was to dump you in the middle of nowhere, then make my escape. Now, I'm angry. Not sure what I'll do." Her voice was getting closer.

"Run while you still can!" Grandma shouted, then clapped a hand over her mouth.

"So, you are close enough to hear me." Susan laughed. "It's almost no challenge at all."

We scuttled backwards, trying to put distance between her and us. I scowled at Grandma. We would be having words later.

Mom tapped my shoulder and pointed to our right. "Cave," she mouthed.

We hurried toward it. If we pulled branches to cover the entrance, we might have a chance at staying hidden. A slim chance, but it was better than nothing. We had a day's supply of water and granola bars. We'd be fine until rescue came.

We each grabbed whatever sticks and brush we could and dragged them with us. Once inside the cave, we positioned them to look as natural as possible.

"Olly olly oxen free!" Susan sang out from further away. "Isn't this fun?"

"She's nuts." Grandma scooted against the far wall.

"Not as crazy as you for giving us away." Mom slapped her shoulder.

"Don't hit your mother." Grandma scowled.

"You could have gotten us killed."

"Hush, both of you." Something moved in the shadows. I shined my cell phone to show a deeper cavern inside this one. "There's something in here with us."

"Lord, have mercy." Grandma pulled Mom in front of her like a shield.

Mom shrugged free. "I think we should take our chances outside."

I agreed. Especially since our company huffed and growled like a large animal. "Let's be quick or else we might be dinner."

Grandma sprinted from the cave. "Slowest person gets eaten, or so they say."

Heart pounding harder than it had since Susan had taken Mom, I joined them outside of the cave. Muffled footsteps and more huffs followed us. I whipped my head from side-to-side. "I think the highway is straight ahead."

"So is Susan," Mom said.

"Yes, but I'm pretty sure we disturbed a bear."

That got them moving. I glanced behind us and we turned and slid down a small hill. A large black bear rose on its hind legs and waved goodbye.

"That animal would make a nice rug," Grandma said.

"For crying out loud." Mom gave her a shove, sending her into a faster pace.

Yep. Would have been better if I was on the run alone.

When we hadn't heard from Susan in a while, we increased our pace, along with the noise and bickering between Mom and Grandma. A person would think that danger wouldn't create tension between two people who usually had none.

"Did Susan ever say why she didn't want the book written?" I asked.

Mom glanced back. "She said it was an embarrassment and Lloyd wouldn't see reason. Then, when Alice found the journal, she needed to stop her from finding out who was behind his death. She knew you were too smart to be killed that way, so she wanted to draw you out. That's why she took me. That, and to keep me from talking. The article never made it into the newspaper." She shrugged. "The gal I gave it to is a cousin of Susan's and was easily persuaded."

"Seems like such a trivial reason to commit murder."

"Not if you're unhinged," Grandma added. "Susan

Hall definitely fits that description. I bet if you looked into her background far enough, she served time in the loony bin."

Which didn't matter at that moment. The only thing that did matter was finding our men and getting the heck out of there…alive.

The sun set early in the woods, and we were plunged suddenly in deep shadows. Never that good with directions in the first place, I was completely discombobulated. We were lost in the woods with wild animals and a crazy woman.

"We're going in circles," Mom said. "We'd better find a place to stop for the night and hope the men find us. As long as we keep moving, we'll pass each other."

"Stop where?" I waved my arm. "It's dark. There are trees everywhere. The only shelter was that bear's home, and he didn't want to share."

Thoroughly discouraged at my failed attempt to find the highway, I plopped on a fallen log and rested my chin on my knees. A dull ache radiated through my foot. My thigh throbbed. My stomach grumbled. I was a mess and wanted Heath's arms around me.

"Toss me a granola bar," Grandma said, holding out her hand. "I can't think when I'm hungry."

I tossed her and Mom one and got one for myself. We sat in the quiet, the only sound was the breeze in the trees and the chomping of our chewing. If not for the circumstances that brought us there, it could have been a peaceful setting.

A twig snapped behind me.

I whirled.

Susan stepped from the bushes, gun drawn. "Well, this is cozy. Seriously, Shelby, I know these woods. I grew up here. My guess is you're lost."

I was not going to admit that she was right. I couldn't have spoken. Instead, I opened my mouth in a silent scream and pointed behind her as a dark, seven foot, shadow rose on two hind legs.

Susan turned and screamed.

25

With one mighty swat of the bear's paw, Susan was face down on the forest floor. Her gun skittered toward me.

I grabbed the gun and tossed it to Grandma. "Shoot."

She jumped back, hands in the air. "I don't know how."

"Good grief." Mom grabbed the gun like a female Dirty Harry.

We riddled the roaring animal with bullets. When it lay dead next to a bleeding, but breathing, Susan, we lowered our weapons.

"Too many holes for a decent rug," Grandma said, standing over the bear, shaking her head.

I rolled my eyes and knelt next to Susan. A large rake of the bear's claws had laid open her uninjured shoulder. I removed my tee shirt and tied it around the wound. "Look at me, Susan. Keep your eyes on my face. Help is coming." I truly hoped the gunshots had alerted Heath and the others to our location.

"Why did you save me?" Tears trickled down Susan's face.

"No one, not even a murderer, deserves to die the way you would have."

"I've been bad, Shelby. All because of my pride." She stared at the night sky. "I deserve to be eaten by a bear. David didn't deserve to die, though. He didn't kill anyone. That was all me. I only asked him to scare you. I really did deserve to be that bear's dinner."

"Don't talk like that." A crashing sounded in the trees. Please be Heath and the others. I was relieved to know they weren't both killers, but David was a guilty as Susan. He could easily have killed me and Cheryl when he ran us off the road.

"It's true. I'm in a lot of pain. Do you think they'll take me to the hospital before carting me off to jail?"

"I'm sure of it."

"Don't worry," Grandma said, patting her shoulder. "I spent time in the slammer. Not for murder, mind you, but it wasn't too unbearable."

Susan chuckled, then her face twisted in pain. "We really could have been friends, old lady."

Grandma frowned. "Not if you call me an old lady, we can't." She marched to Mom's side as Heath and the others entered the small clearing.

Heath cast a sharp glance at the dead bear, then rushed to my side. "Are you all right?"

I nodded, wrapping my arms tightly around his waist. "We need an ambulance for Susan." Now that the danger was past, my legs lost their strength and I sagged against him.

Heath scooped me in his arms, then sat on the log I'd vacated what seemed years ago. "Who killed the animal?"

"Mom and I did. We disturbed its slumber." I rested my cheek against his chest while Ted, Seth, and two officers I didn't know tended to Susan.

I was glad the bear hadn't killed her. A horrible thing to watch, much less experience. Justice would be served behind bars. That was enough for me.

"Did she say why she did it?"

"Embarassment." I closed my eyes. "A simple desire to protect the family name."

"I guess that means a whole lot to certain people." He stood, still holding me. "Let's go home and snuggle on the couch."

"That's the best thing I've heard all day." I gave a sad smile at the thought Cheryl wasn't going to be happy about missing the excitement. But, she wasn't a nature gal and would have balked at traipsing through the woods. It was better that she was safely in a classroom with twenty-five eight-year-olds.

I glanced at Mom and Grandma, wishing they hadn't had to come along. "Mom, where did you learn to shoot like that?"

She grinned. "Your father used to take me to the shooting range with him. I'm glad I haven't lost my touch. Of course, that bear was the largest thing I've ever had to shoot." Her smile faded. "So sad. It was such a magnificent animal."

"Do you think I could have the claws for earrings?" Grandma asked. "I know this guy—"

"Let it be." I caressed Heath's face. "You said

something about snuggling?"

~

Back at the cottage, Mom made coffee and handed us each one. Seth had sent the two officers I didn't know home and now perched on the coffee table, his gaze locked on mine. "Susan Hall is a former mental patient—"

"I told you!" Grandma gave a fist bump to the air. "Didn't I tell you?"

Seth glanced heavenward and shook his head. "She escaped. I'll be speaking with Alice about a more in-depth hiring process."

"If that was the case, she never would have hired me." I grinned over the rim of my mug. "I had absolutely no experience."

"Well, you have plenty now. I'm not sure the department could have figured this out without the help you gave us."

"What about the mayor?" Heath asked.

"Completely innocent of involvement and thoroughly embarrassed at another mark to his family name. But…" Seth smiled. "He has promised not to retaliate."

"That's good news." I propped my foot on the coffee table. "I left my boot somewhere in the woods."

"It's probably time to take it off anyway," Heath said. "We'll call your doctor, just to make sure."

"You should have seen my girl." Mom perched on the arm of the sofa and put her arm around me. "She was a true sergeant, leading her troops to safety, barking orders. It wasn't until you showed up, Heath, that she got weak."

My face heated.

"I like it when she leans on me." Heath winked.

Bob, Mom's squeeze, burst into my cottage and made a beeline for my mother. He grabbed her into his arms and gave her a very heated kiss.

My eyes widened, and my face grew hotter.

"I'm so sorry I was gone, Sue Ellen," he said. "I would have stormed the gates of hell to protect you."

"I know, dear. But, I'm fine. Come. Let me get you some coffee."

"How do you feel about that?" Heath asked, motioning his head toward the couple.

"I'm not sure. I think I'm okay, but Bob isn't Dad. It's more important that Mom is happy. She deserves a man who loves her." I put his arm around my shoulders. "Snuggle, remember?" I didn't care that the cottage was full of people. The only thing that mattered was that I was surrounded by my family, the people I loved, and everyone was safe.

I raised my eyes. *Thank you, God.* Maybe it was time to start talking to him again.

"That was our biggest adventure yet," Grandma said. "And I didn't have to fake a heart attack. Shelby got away slick as a snake."

"You and your adventures." Ted tapped her on the nose. "You're giving me grey hairs."

"Your head was full when we met. Don't blame that on me, you old coot." Grandma sighed and rested her head on his shoulder. "Seth, maybe you should talk to Cheryl about moving in here. You're the only one without your love."

"We haven't talked about love." He bolted to his feet. "I've got reports to write." He ran out as if he were being chased by something big and hairy.

Heath laughed. "Poor fool doesn't know what he's missing." His hold tightened. "I'm glad to have you back, Shelby."

"I tried to think of a reason I might commit murder, you know, without my life, or a loved one's, being in danger, and I can't come up with a single reason. It's mind boggling how some people are triggered to kill by simple things in their life."

"That's one of the evils of living in this world," Ted said. "It's all around us. The world needs more people willing to stand up for justice. You did good, Shelby. Have you considered joining the police force?"

I jerked. "No way. I've seen the physical training y'all go through, and I'm not interested." I might be able to get over a big wall if something was chasing me, but I doubted it. "I'll keep sticking my nose where it doesn't belong, and be content." I grinned. "Someone has to keep y'all's lives interesting."

"True," Heath said. "But do you have to scare the wits out of me on a regular basis?"

"Keeping you on your toes, handsome."

"Let's have a few months of boredom, okay?"

I glanced up at him. "You got it. Nothing until Christmas, I promise."

"Great. I get four months."

"That's a hard promise, Shelby." Grandma's brows lowered in puzzlement. "How can you promise that no murders or thefts will take place? Weren't you listening to a thing Teddy said? Bad things are all around us."

"I can try, Grandma. I can certainly try." I closed my eyes, content to sleep on Heath's shoulder for the rest of my life.

I smiled. I'd done it again. I'd solved another

murder and lived to tell about it.
How long could this streak of luck continue?

The End

Scan the code to learn more about the next book,
Poinsettia Madness

ABOUT THE AUTHOR

www.cynthiahickey.com

Cynthia Hickey is a multi-published and best-selling author of cozy mysteries and romantic suspense. She has taught writing at many conferences and small writing retreats. She and her husband run the publishing press, Winged Publications. They live in Arizona and Arkansas, becoming snowbirds with three dogs. They have ten grandchildren who keep them busy and tell everyone they know that "Nana is a writer."

www.ingramcontent.com/pod-product-compliance
Lightning Source LLC
Chambersburg PA
CBHW070259120726
47910CB00007B/2308